Coming soon in
THE LEAGUE OF SECRET HEROES:

THE LEAGUE OF SECRET HEROES

Cape

Book One

By KATE HANNIGAN
Illustrated by PATRICK SPAZIANTE

Aladdin
New York London Toronto Sydney New Delhi

This book is a work of fiction. Any references to historical events, real people, or real places are used fictitiously. Other names, characters, places, and events are products of the author's imagination, and any resemblance to actual events or places or persons, living or dead, is entirely coincidental.

ALADDIN
An imprint of Simon & Schuster Children's Publishing Division
1230 Avenue of the Americas, New York, New York 10020
First Aladdin hardcover edition August 2019
Text copyright © 2019 by Kate Hannigan
Jacket illustration copyright © 2019 by Kelsey Eng
Interior illustrations copyright © 2019 by Patrick Spaziante
All rights reserved, including the right of reproduction in whole or in part in any form.
ALADDIN and related logo are registered trademarks of Simon & Schuster, Inc.
For information about special discounts for bulk purchases, please contact
Simon & Schuster Special Sales at 1-866-506-1949 or business@simonandschuster.com.
The Simon & Schuster Speakers Bureau can bring authors to your live event. For
more information or to book an event contact the Simon & Schuster Speakers Bureau
at 1-866-248-3049 or visit our website at www.simonspeakers.com.
Jacket designed by Laura Lyn DiSiena and Sammy Yuen Jr.
Interior designed by Laura Lyn DiSiena
The illustrations for this book were rendered digitally.
The text of this book was set in Marion.
Manufactured in the United States of America 0619 FFG
2 4 6 8 10 9 7 5 3 1
Library of Congress Cataloging-in-Publication Data
Names: Hannigan, Kate, author. | Spaziante, Patrick, illustrator.
Title: Cape / by Kate Hannigan ; illustrated by Patrick Spaziante.
Description: First Aladdin hardcover edition. | New York : Aladdin, 2019. |
Series: The League of Secret Heroes ; [1] | Includes bibliographical references. | Summary:
Soon after being recruited by the mysterious Mrs. Boudica to join a secret military
intelligence operation, Josie, Mae, and Akiko discover their superhero abilites and use
them to thwart a Nazi plot to steal the ENIAC computer.
Identifiers: LCCN 2018037398 (print) | LCCN 2018043918 (eBook) |
ISBN 9781534439139 (eBook) | ISBN 9781534439115 (hc)
Subjects: | CYAC: Superheroes—Fiction. | Secrets—Fiction. | Spies—Fiction. |
Computers—Fiction. | World War, 1939–1945—United States—Fiction.
Classification: LCC PZ7.H198158 (eBook) | LCC PZ7.H198158 Cap 2019 (print) |
DDC [Fic]—dc23
LC record available at https://lccn.loc.gov/2018037398

For Mom and Dad,
my first superheroes

One

Two

WHEN THE WORLD NEEDS A HERO, SOME-times you have to become one.

That was my mom's thinking. And it seemed simple enough that even knuckleheads like my brothers, Vinnie and Baby Lou, could understand. Because Mam did that kind of thing all the time. Like when she made corned beef sandwiches for the family next door when she saw they couldn't pay for groceries, or gave away one of her best dresses to the neighbor whose husband died fighting the Nazis—so the lady would have something decent to wear to his funeral.

For my little family, the whole world was basically our third-floor apartment. The one above Mr. Hunter's barbershop on Captain Flexor Street in West Philadelphia, between the cleaners and the weeping willow tree. And as Mam liked to say, I was the hero of it.

That's because my taking a job at Gerda's Diner down the block helped pay the rent each month, which kept us from getting kicked out onto the street.

Which made my little brother Vinnie stop tugging on that clump of hair above his forehead and worrying all the time.

Which made my mom able to breathe.

But let's be honest here. Clearing the diner's tables of lipstick-smudged coffee cups and dirty plates stuck with scrambled eggs? That didn't feel too heroic to me.

It wasn't anything like the superheroes from years past— the ones who soared over rooftops and battled villains to save our city. Using superstrength to stop a speeding train from crashing off a bridge? Protecting a bunch of innocent people from harm? Now, those were things heroes did. And people loved them so much for it, they named schools and parks and streets after them.

Nobody's naming anything after me.

Lately I've started wondering where all the superheroes have gone. Because with the war on, we sure could use a few of them flying around, all billowy capes and mysterious masks over their eyes and shiny boots. The papers and radio reports haven't had much news about superheroes, not since the war's fighting turned really bad.

Some people even stopped believing in them. Superheroes were becoming just bedtime stories parents told their kids, like tales of King Arthur or leprechauns or the tooth fairy. Others started thinking they were just made-up characters in comic books—not real people trying to do good.

I couldn't bear the thought. I told myself all the superheroes were off in the Pacific Ocean fighting the Japanese alongside our troops there. And over in Europe battling back against Germany's Nazis. But to be perfectly honest, part of me was starting to worry they'd hung up their capes and decided to wait for better times.

This was the argument Emmett and I were having last night at my kitchen table over plates of Spam hash. We were supposed to be doing homework, but we kept getting distracted.

"Face it, Josie," he was saying. "The caped heroes of your beloved comic books are history. Done, finished, behind us. If you keep going on about them, people are going to think you're crazy."

"I'm not crazy, Emmett Shea, and you know it." My voice cut through the usual noise in our apartment—over the radio, my brothers' Parcheesi game, my cousin's sewing machine, and my mother's teakettle. "Superheroes are still out there saving people's lives and rescuing dogs and stopping evildoers. They're just quiet, for some reason. It's probably the war. Or the heat this summer . . ."

Emmett gave me a doubtful look. He didn't even need to say what he was thinking. That's because we both knew that superheroes had been quiet for longer than just the past couple of weeks, when the weather had started heating up. More like the past couple of years. When I really thought about it, superheroes hadn't been spotted in Philadelphia since I was in fourth or fifth grade.

"Hurry up and guess, Emmett," I groused, pointing at his pencil. I wasn't annoyed with the time Emmett was taking to solve my puzzle. It was his attitude about superheroes that bothered me. "You've stared at those clues long enough."

"Don't rush me, Josie," he said, unfazed by my crankiness. Nothing could ruffle Emmett's feathers. Especially when he was puzzling. "And don't be salty with me over superheroes quitting. Hauntima, Hopscotch, Nova the Sunchaser—even that favorite pair of yours, those sisters Zenobia and the Palomino. They must figure there's a whole bunch of puzzle solvers and other smarties like you and me coming to take their jobs. So they quit."

He gave me a smirk, then stared harder at the clues I'd laid out for him.

175, 21, 5–6

7, 5, 8

34, 12, 1

306, 21, 5

287, 4, 4

"I don't think it's an alphabet cipher, since some of these numbers are higher than twenty-six," Emmett mumbled, thinking out loud. "So maybe a book cipher?"

I dropped my pencil onto the paper and groaned. He was almost too good at this! I'd have to read up on harder puzzles so I could really stump him next time.

"Hmmm. What book would you choose?" His eyes scanned the kitchen shelves, searching the spines of Mam's cookbooks. I kept my eyes on my homework sheet, trying not to give myself away. Because in the doorway to the dining room, just beside the radio, sat a stack of my favorite books.

"Aha!" Emmett shouted, pouncing on them. "It's got to be one of these."

He scooped up the stack and plunked it down on the table, jolting our pencils and papers. Then he arranged my books in a row, side by side, so he could read each title plainly.

"No fair, Josie. Book ciphers are only good when we have the exact same book. That way we each can look up the pages."

I shrugged and gave him a look, trying hard not to let him catch me smiling.

"If you can't figure it out, Emmett, don't start whining. A puzzle's a puzzle. Maybe mine are just too hard for you. . . ."

That did the trick.

"Nobody is saying your puzzles are too hard, Josie. Now, let's see—what would you choose for your book cipher? *Mr. Popper's Penguins*? *Little House on the Prairie*? *The Boxcar Children*?"

I tapped my pencil on my teacup and pretended not to hear him. He'd have to figure this out on his own. No hints from me.

"Come on, Josie, help me! Just a teeny-tiny clue."

I pointed at the rows of numbers and reminded him that I'd given him five clues already. But Emmett was desperate.

"I've got to be home before my mom gets off her shift. So give a guy a break, Josie. Which book did you choose? I can solve it from there."

I tapped my temple and teased Emmett just a little bit more.

"Think about it," I began, pretending exasperation. "One of these books has the greatest redhead of all time! In all of literature! How can you ask me, of all people, which book I'd pick?"

Emmett stared at my raging-red curls, and now it was his turn for exasperation.

"*Anne of Green Gables!*" he hollered, slapping his hand

onto the cover of the last book and whipping it open. "I should have known you'd choose this one. But it's a little predictable, Josie, when you think about it."

"Well, clearly you didn't think about it, now, did you?"

Turning the pages, counting down the lines, then over the right number of words, Emmett solved my cipher in a matter of seconds.

"Okay, the first clue is on page 175," he mumbled, double-checking himself, "twenty-first line, the fifth and sixth words. 'Second shelf.'"

"And the whole puzzle reads?"

Emmett cleared his throat and tried to sound like a master puzzler.

"Your cipher, Miss Know-It-All Josephine O'Malley, reads: 'Second shelf behind you red box.'"

He waited just a beat or two, staring at me. Then the meaning sank in. And Emmett jumped to his feet, raced to the second shelf of the pantry just behind his chair, and grabbed the red tin cookie box with the Lorna Doone label. I'd just refilled it that afternoon.

"Shortbread cookies! My favorite!"

"Zenobia could have solved that faster," I pointed out. "Or the Palomino, Hauntima, Hopscotch, Nova the Sunchaser . . ."

Three

*E*MMETT HAD MADE IT CLEAR LAST NIGHT over homework and puzzling that he didn't believe there were superheroes around anymore. But I sure did. That's because I needed them—a lot. So as I stood there in front of Gerda's Diner, my cheeks burned hot, and my hands shook with anger. Toby's team of bullies couldn't even ride the bikes they'd stolen from my little brothers—their legs were too long. They'd probably just give them to the youngest of their lunkhead gang, Toby's bullies-in-training.

Toby must have seen my outrage, because he took off running just as I lunged for him. Toby was bigger than me but clumsy. So when I whipped my broom out ahead of me and caught his feet, I sent him spilling onto the sidewalk.

The anger inside me made me want to pounce, claws bared. Instead, as he rolled over to face me, I pressed the handle of the broom to his chest, in the little round spot just between his collarbones. He gasped, but I'd caught his attention.

"I've had it with you, Toby," I said, my voice tight, my heart pounding in my chest. "Why can't you leave us alone?"

Toby's taunting had been easy enough to ignore at first. Mam was always reminding us not to pay any mind to the unkind things people sometimes said. *Cruelty comes from weakness*, she'd tell me and my brothers. *People who feel weak want to find somebody to look down on. But they're already in the mud and the muck—don't let them pull you down with them.*

Hands shaking, I gripped the broomstick tighter and stared down at Toby's arrogant smirk. Weakness? Who did Mam think felt weak? Toby? Leader of our neighborhood bullies? The kid with the bossy dad who seemed to run our whole block?

Toby and his beady-eyed buddies liked to tease me on the monkey bars at recess, whenever they caught me singing songs from back home in Ireland. *Speak American!* they'd shout. *Or go back to where you came from.*

"I'm warning you, Josie O'Malley," Toby growled now, wrapping his hands around the broomstick and trying to push me back. "My dad won't like hearing about this."

"He'll tell on you, Josie," said Vinnie, his words high-pitched and panicky. "It's not worth it!"

"Mam won't like it one bit," added Baby Lou. I could tell he was near tears, though he'd never let Toby Hunter see him cry.

Mam.

I squeezed my eyes shut and tried to bottle up my rage.

Mam couldn't take one more thing.

Toby's loudmouthed father ran the barbershop downstairs, and he owned our whole building. If Toby told his dad on me—conveniently leaving out the parts about stealing my brothers' bikes and lunches, and their confidence, too—Mr. Hunter would never listen to my side of things. He'd kick my family out of the apartment. And that would be too much for my mom to take.

Especially now, since the news about Dad.

"Be safe," she'd told me this morning, her words part whispered prayer, part command. "Mind yourself, Josie. I can't bear anything happening to you or the boys. Or to Kay. I can't lose you."

Be safe. No trouble. Come straight home. Mam needed us to live like mice, scurrying here and there without drawing attention to ourselves. And I had promised her that's what I'd do—so help me, Toby Hunter.

I would not steal his bike right back, just to make things even.

I would not tell on him to the cops or to my teachers.

I would not punch his splotchy pink face, even though I wanted to so badly, it made my palms itch.

But the puzzler tryout? Now, that's something I wasn't about to give up. Even though my mom wanted us staying inside the apartment and practically wrapping ourselves in pillows, I refused to walk away from this chance. Math games, word games, solving ciphers—all these things came easy to me.

Getting this puzzler job would be my own way of fighting the war, small as it seemed. For Dad, who'd been fighting since the Japanese bombed Pearl Harbor. For Mam, who worked a second job putting battleships together at the shipyard. For my little brothers and Cousin Kay.

I was willing to walk away from battles with Toby, like Mam wanted. But not the war.

I lifted the broomstick and stepped aside.

"Off to school now," I snapped to Vinnie and Baby Lou. I could hardly look at them. The mixture of shame and embarrassment made the broom weigh heavy, like it was made of iron instead of wood. My arms sagged. "You've got to run or you'll be late. Go!"

For once in their lives, my knucklehead little brothers did what I asked of them.

Choking and sputtering, Toby got to his feet.

"Smart move for such a stupid girl. I'd hate to have to tell my dad we're renting to a bully."

And he let out a laugh, a deep and dangerous guffaw that hit me like a fist to my stomach. It lingered menacingly behind him as he swaggered off after his thieving buddies.

I turned back toward the diner, past the wirehaired dog barking on his leash, and glanced up at the well-dressed owner holding the newspaper. She was looking at me now, reading my face like it was one of those news stories. I wondered what she'd caught of the fight between Toby and me.

Stupid. Is there a more hurtful word in the English language?

I glanced up and saw my reflection in the diner window: curly hair corkscrewing in every direction, faded dungarees needing a wash, loose white blouse making me look scrawnier than I already was.

Stupid girl.

Was I foolish to try out for the puzzler job? Was it ridiculous to think I was a math whiz like my cousin Kay? I swallowed hard, trying to push the doubts away. But maybe Toby Hunter was right. Maybe I was just a stupid girl.

And what good was a stupid girl to anybody? Especially one who couldn't even save a couple of red bikes.

"Hey, Josie!"

The shout came from the other side of the dog and his owner. It was Emmett. He was a little breathless as he trotted over, his usual cheerful smile replaced by a scowl.

"That Toby Hunter." He shook his head, and his eyebrows formed a deep V. Clearly he'd run into my brothers on their way to school. "He's had a grudge against you ever since that math contest last year. You made him look bad. Scratch that—he made himself look bad, since he's nothing but oatmeal up there." And he knocked his knuckles on his forehead.

I shrugged and stared down at the sidewalk, kicking at a bottle cap. What was I supposed to do against a grudge? People made no sense to me sometimes. Maybe that's why I liked puzzles and math so much—they were things I *could* figure out.

And they never made me feel like I did right now. Stupid.

"I can't do anything to stop him," I said, fighting the urge to snap my broomstick. "Punks like Toby can do whatever they want. And people like me just have to live with it."

"Don't underestimate yourself, Josie," Emmett said. "You may feel like you're powerless right now. But things can change."

I looked away, suddenly wanting to hide behind my broom.

"Listen, about your brothers' bikes," Emmett went on. "I'll try to help you get them back. But don't do it alone, Josie. Toby can make things really bad for you."

I nodded. I really did need somebody like Emmett on my

side—brains as well as kindness. A little like Zenobia, my all-time favorite of the superheroes. I put my hand on my comic book in my back pocket. Zenobia's powers, like heat beams and levitation and superstrength, were amazing, but what I liked best about her was that she used her superpowers to help people. And not just here in Philadelphia but around the country too.

That is, before she and the other superheroes stopped showing up.

"*He meets Mat?*" I asked Emmett, feeling a little better about things.

"You know it," he answered, a grin breaking out on his goofy face. And then he threw an easy punch at my shoulder. "*I help lonesome Jay?*"

A laugh pawed at my stomach like a playful puppy. That's because Emmett and I were using our secret codes. *He meets Mat* was Emmett's name—Emmett Shea—with the letters scrambled up like a plate of diner eggs. And *I help lonesome Jay* was mine—Josephine O'Malley.

Emmett and I had started rearranging the letters in names and places to pass time during our boring classes last year. We liked to slip each other notes in our secret jumbled language so nobody knew what we were talking about.

Solving each other's puzzles was just for laughs at first. But as the school year wore on and things got harder for both of us, we came to depend on our notes back and forth.

And when nothing else made sense—not our parents, our friends, or this terrible war—we both knew we could count on each other to help unscramble things.

"Thanks," I called after Emmett as he hurried off. "I needed that!" He waved and shouted something about catching up with me later over milkshakes. I watched as the stream of people passing on the sidewalk swept him up, his brown head bobbing along with the others on their morning commute.

But as I waved after him, I noticed Emmett wasn't headed toward our school. He was trudging off in the opposite direction. And it suddenly occurred to me that Emmett Shea must be up to something, but he hadn't let me in on his secret.

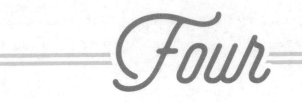

Four

"WHY THE SCOWL, JOSIE?"

The door to the diner opened, and Harry Sawyer, who helped Gerda run things, nodded for me to come back inside. My frustration with Toby must have shown on my face.

"I've never heard you say a bad word to anyone," he said, reaching a hand up to quiet the tinkling bell that hung above the door. "What's put a flea in your ear?"

"Meanies," I said, using one of Baby Lou's words. "Bullies, brutes, tough guys, lunkheads. Whatever you want to call them."

Harry let out a sigh and took the broom from my hand. "Well, from what I saw, you were a bit unkind yourself."

"Toby Hunter made me do it! Did you hear him? He was teasing Baby Lou, and then he sto—"

Tut-tut-tut. Harry made a clicking noise that cut me off. "Don't blame someone else. I expect more from you, Josie. We all do."

"Maybe I shouldn't have poked him with my broom," I mumbled, grabbing a few orders from the counter and getting ready to carry them over to the tables. "But I tell you what, Harry, I'm not going to stay quiet anymore. I can't."

Harry shook his head, clearly disappointed in me. "You can't lash out like that. Use your brains, Josie. Don't outrage an opponent, out*smart* them—like that caped hero you're always going on about. What's her name?"

"Zenobia," I answered, happy to note that Harry had been paying attention to our conversations. "Zenobia could outsmart anyone in the universe. But since she's gone missing for so long now, people are starting to wonder if she was even real. If superheroes are even real."

"We have a saying in Germany: *Selbst ist die Frau.* 'You're the woman. It's up to you.' Not your friends or your family or your favorite superhero. You're the one who decides what kind of person you'll be, Josie. Someone who follows her temper and chooses to be cruel? Or someone who chooses to be kind?"

He shoved my broom into the closet, then turned to the sink to wash up. "*Selbst ist die Frau.* You're the one, pal."

The morning rush was on, so I delivered the plates of eggs and pancakes where they needed to go. Usually, I'd be hurrying out the door for school. But today I had time to make the rounds of the tables—pouring coffee into cups, clearing dirty dishes into the sink—and replay this morning's fight in my mind.

When I circled back to the long white counter half an hour or so later, Gerda was behind it sorting silverware. Harry came over to join us, slipping a fresh-baked pie under the glass dome of a display plate.

Gerda's cuckoo clock on the wall above our heads began its hourly routine, chiming nine times.

"It's already nine o'clock? I have to take off in a couple minutes," I said, climbing onto one of the high stools.

I pulled my comic book from the pocket of my dungarees, along with a newspaper clipping tucked inside it, and laid them on the counter. Unfolding the clipping and smoothing the creases flat, I pointed to the important details.

"This is where I'm going today. I cut it out of the *Inquirer*," I said, my voice a little hushed. The newspaper felt like a pirate's map, and I was pointing to the treasure. "Look right here. It's an advertisement for puzzlers. The government needs puzzle experts to help fight the Nazis. And that's me!"

"It *is* you, Josie," said Gerda, leaning in closer to read the fine print. I inhaled her fresh-baked-bread smell and tried to make the irritation of the morning disappear. "Look what it says: 'Are you a pro with puzzles? A wonder with words? A master at mathematics?' They'd be lucky to have you!"

My eyes devoured the advertisement again. Here was my big chance. I was too puny to enlist in the army—plus, as a girl, I wouldn't get past the first doctor's exam. And I was too young to get a job in an aircraft factory and build planes like Rosie the Riveter. Or at the naval shipyard and build battleships like Wendy the Welder and my mom.

But puzzling? This was the job for me.

"I'll try to come back in time for the supper rush," I said, scooping up the clipping and my comic book and leaping off the high stool. "And I promise not to quit my job here, no matter what they pay me as a puzzler!"

Gerda laughed as she wiped up the countertop, wishing me luck. And Harry tapped his temple again and called after me.

"It's up to you," he said with an encouraging wave. "You're the one, pal!"

Five

J COULDN'T HIDE THE LITTLE SKIP IN MY step as I headed off toward the Carson Building. The newspaper advertisement was meant exactly for me. I just knew it. I'd spent years playing math games and word scrambles, and Emmett and I had egged each other on to make our messages more complicated and harder to solve.

"*He meets Mat,*" I mumbled. "*She met mate.*" A grin took over my face at the thought of Emmett and our scrambled names. I couldn't help but mix up the letters a few more times. "*Sam met thee. She ate temm. . . .*"

"Sam? Mat?" came a voice suddenly beside me. "Are they friends of yours?"

Whipping my head around, I discovered my cousin Kay McNulty. She nudged me playfully with her left shoulder as she bit into what looked like an apple turnover. The flaky pastry crumbs scattered behind us in the breeze as we made our way down the block together.

"You look hungry," I said, dusting a few flakes from her pretty blue jacket. Kay was good at sewing, and she made the most beautiful clothes. "Are you heading into work or just getting off?"

"*Mhhst httng fff,*" she answered. Then, after a moment to chew, she translated: "Just getting off. I'm starving. It was another late night—so exhausting, but so interesting. I'm going to sleep for a few hours, then head back in again this evening."

I wasn't exactly sure what Kay did. Mam told my brothers and me once that it had something to do with a nearby store, Caruso's Market. I think Kay's job was to ring up groceries— apples and milk and bread and things.

I'd never really thought about it. Funny that she'd find a cashier's job "so interesting." Or that it would sometimes keep her up all night and through to the morning.

"Hey," I began slowly, "why is it you work so many hours when—"

But Kay jumped in with her own questions.

"Where are you off to, my dear young cousin? You don't appear to be headed for school. Are you playing hooky?

Skipping the last few days before summer vacation?" And in a low voice she added, "Does your mother know?"

I couldn't stop the laugh that bubbled up. Kay lived with us and helped Mam pay the rent—just like I did with money I earned from Gerda's Diner. Kay may have been only a cousin, but I loved her like a sister. And while she was a puzzle solver like me, she was much better. Kay was a mathematician, with a college diploma framed on the wall and everything.

And a mathematician was great to have around when I needed help with homework.

"Mam knows I want to try out. She just doesn't know exactly when," I explained, hiding my smile. "I want to surprise her."

She raised a single eyebrow.

"The tryout," I reminded her, another skip in my step. "Don't you remember, Kay? I've only talked about it a hundred times. The puzzler tryout is today—this morning—at the Carson Building. I'm heading over now."

"Right-e-o!" she said, jumping over a low garden railing to reach a trash can. "You'll do great, Josie!" Kay was always jumping over things, from fences to park benches to garden sheds. They were never obstacles to her, just little diversions along her path. Kay was funny that way.

But she wasn't exactly funny. Kay had a look about her that was all business: tallish with high cheekbones and fast blue eyes. Her brown hair had a shimmery, golden quality. And the way she carried herself reminded me of my favorite movie star, Katharine Hepburn.

What I loved best about Kay was the way her mind worked. Her thoughts seemed to speed along about twenty miles per hour faster than most people's, which made anyone speaking with her have to run to keep up. And which made good entertainment for me, Vinnie, and Baby Lou when she got going. Smart and tough, that was Kay's way.

"Keep focused, Josie. No distractions!"

But there was a softness to Kay too. She was patient and kind and always encouraging. Maybe it was all that sewing she did that made her so calm, taking each part of it step by step by step. Collars, sleeves, buttonholes. One stitch at a time. That's how she helped me with my math homework: *Take it one step at a time, Josie. Did you do the first thing correctly? The second?*

Or it could have been her Girl Scout training that made Kay so patient and encouraging, working with little pain-in-the-neck kids like my brothers and me. Whatever it was, I adored Kay. And when she headed out the apartment door in her sharp work clothes, her hat a bright blue or a vivid red, she seemed fearless—like the best comic book heroes all wrapped up in one person.

Kay was the whole reason I thought I could even be picked as a puzzler.

"Okay, Josie, impress me," she urged. "Get me from *cat* to *dog* in three steps. Go!"

"That's easy." I smiled. "Let's see. Swap the *A*, and *cat* becomes *cot*. Flip the *C*, and *cot* turns to *dot*. Change the *T*, and *dot* becomes *dog*!"

She nodded her approval.

"Not bad," she said as we quickened our pace. "But keep in mind they might throw trickier bits at you: complicated sequences, codes, patterns, odd-one-outs."

"I've got this, Kay. No problem," I said, tucking in the tail of my white blouse with GERDA'S DINER embroidered in bright green thread. Hopefully I sounded confident. I just needed Toby Hunter's voice to stop playing over and over again in my head.

Stupid girl.

"I've got as good a chance as anyone else," I whispered. "Right?"

As we reached the fancy revolving doors of the Carson Building, Kay turned to face me. She wasn't one for hugs or making a big to-do. So when she focused her eyes on mine, I couldn't help but pay close attention.

"Now listen, Josie. You can do anything you set your mind to." Kay peered down into my face, our noses inches apart, and I could see the fine needlework she'd sewn at her collar. "You just have to approach it in a deliberate way. Stitch by stitch by stitch.

"Got it?"

"I—I do, Kay," I stuttered a little self consciously. Kay seemed to have faith in my abilities, even when I wasn't so sure. "Stitch by stitch by stitch."

She smiled and gave a quick nod, her eyes encouraging. "Every problem has a solution. Just remember that."

I gave her the most confident smile I could muster. Then, at the last second, I threw my arms around her shoulders and squeezed as tight as I could, stealing a hug before racing through the revolving wood-and-glass doors and into the Carson Building's lobby. I wanted to bottle up Kay's confidence and hold on to it.

"Thanks, Kay." And throwing one of her own favorite expressions over my shoulder, I called, "Right-e-o!"

Six

I WAS THE FIRST ONE TO FINISH THE EXAM, so I walked up to the instructor's desk and set my paper down. He slid it to his left, then let out a sniff that, I quickly realized, meant I should go sit down again.

When I got back to my desk, I stared up the row at him. Hank Hissler was his name, and he wore round wire glasses that made him look like a professor. His mustache sat above his lip in a perfectly straight, thin line—like something I could have drawn with a pencil. And his bald head was round as a grapefruit, ending in a pointed chin where a deep dimple in the middle looked like a baby's bottom.

The thought of it made me laugh, which I wasn't supposed to be doing. I clamped a hand over my mouth to trap it. But still, it fizzed up like soda in a bottle that's been shaken.

After a moment or two, the mouth breather seated behind me got up to turn in her exam. I'd listened to her noisy wheezing for the past two hours, so I didn't exactly smile as she passed me by.

Ah-choo!

A mouth breather and a sneezer.

I watched as two boys got up from different sides of the room and reached the instructor's desk at the same time. Mr. Hissler took their exams and placed them in a pile on his right side.

The girl seated just beside me got up next, and she walked up the aisle to Mr. Hissler's desk like she was in church. With a curtsy that seemed overly formal, she passed him her test. I watched Mr. Hissler add it to the left-hand stack—the one that had my exam and the mouth breather's. Three more boys turned in theirs, and he put them in the right-hand pile.

What happened next made me rub my eyes, just to make sure I wasn't seeing things. Because that Mr. Hissler put one hand on the left-side pile, and he slid it into the garbage can at the same time as he took two more exams from a couple of gangly boys. He added theirs to the remaining pile, the one on the right side.

"Hank Hissler, what is happening in this room?"

He jumped as if there were a buzzer in the seat of his chair. And whirling around, he faced an angry figure standing in the doorway, her arms planted on her hips. I might not have recognized her at first if it hadn't been for the brown-and-white dog who trotted in beside her. That dog looked like Astra.

They were the pair from the diner this morning!

"Mrs. Boudica! No need for alarm," he said, though he was clearly alarmed. He seemed to be caught doing something he wasn't supposed to be. "Just a quick exam for my next project."

"Your project? Why haven't I been informed about *your* project?"

"I'm sure I told you about it," he said, scooping up the tests turned in by the men and boys and tucking them into a leather briefcase. "Now, applicants," he called out, addressing the rest of us, "thank you for your time. Should Room Twelve need your services, we will be in touch. Good day. The elevators to the lobby are down the hall and to the right."

Slowly we looked around the room, all of us a bit stunned. I knew I'd done well on this test. Really well. But was that Mr. Hissler even going to consider my exam? Should I race to the trash can and pull it out? Shove it into his hands?

And what did he mean by "room twelve"? I'd touched the brass numbers on the door myself when I'd arrived. We were in room seven forty-five.

"Josie!" hollered a familiar voice. "What are you doing here?"

I turned in time to see Emmett filing toward the door with some of the other test takers—a couple of white-haired men, a woman who looked a little bit like my mom, and another boy of about sixteen. They all handed in their tests to Mr. Hissler as they passed up the aisle. Mrs. Boudica glared.

"Well, of course you're here," Emmett said, answering his own question with a goofy shrug as more test takers pushed out of the room. I laughed, realizing his secret morning appointment had been the same as mine. "You'd make a perfect puzzler! We can talk later today—same time, same place!"

I waved goodbye as he headed down the hall with the others. On my feet now, I gazed over at this Mrs. Boudica and her dog, who seemed to be growling at Mr. Hissler's knees. Should I tell her what happened to my exam? And to the other female test takers?

I took a few timid steps toward them, but as I got closer, Mr. Hissler looked up from his stack of tests and eyed me. He was wearing his hat now, a gray fedora with a black band. The brim looked stiff and somehow dangerous, glinting like a razor's edge.

"You there," he snapped, his yellowish eyes locking on mine. "I have a question. You were speaking to that young man. Does he go by the name"—and he looked down at the top exam, then back at me—"Emmett Shea? Quite bright, that one. I'd like to catch up with him."

Mr. Hissler held me in his snakelike gaze. I was mesmerized, paralyzed. I stared back at him, unable to utter a word.

"You seem to be an acquaintance of his. Is that right?" And now Mr. Hissler attempted to smile. Evidently it was not something he did very often, so the effort looked painful. "Perhaps you could tell me how to find him?"

I glanced beside me, at the mouth breather, who seemed too stunned to walk away from the desks, and at the overly polite curtsy dropper. We were the last three people from the puzzle tryout left in the room, besides the wirehaired pooch and his owner.

"Emmett Shea's not just an acquaintance. He's my best friend," I said, a little unsure of how many beans I wanted to spill. I was thinking about my exam in his trash can. "So I know where and when anybody can find Emmett. We have milkshakes together at five o'clock every afternoon— root beer floats with chocolate ice cream, to be exact. I know because I make them myself."

I hiked up the waistband of my dungarees and tried to look confident. But my knees were starting to shake as this Mr. Hissler kept his beady eyes on me.

"And where is this milkshake establishment, miss?"

I gulped. Now Mrs. Boudica was staring at me too. And she was pretty angry-looking as well, though I couldn't tell if she was mad at me and the last two test takers or only at this Mr. Hissler, who seemed to have gone behind her back about something.

"After the way you treated our tests today," I said, nodding toward the trash can, "I don't think it would be right for me to tell you where to find him. You might have to puzzle that out yourself. Sir."

He gave another little sniff. Then he shoved a few more puzzler exams into his briefcase, flipped a latch to fasten it, and tugged down the brim of that dangerous-looking fedora hat. In an instant, he disappeared through the door without another word. I wanted to grab my exam and wave it after him, but there was no need. Mrs. Boudica had already plucked it out of the trash, along with the other ones.

"Hmmm." She turned them over, studying our work.

"*Pfff.*" She sniffed, then went on reading.

"Well," she finally said.

I peeked over at the mouth breather, who peered at the curtsy dropper. What were we supposed to make of this lady?

Finally, her dog let out a few barks and raced around us.

"Good work, girls." Mrs. Boudica smiled, tucking the exams under her arm and calling to Astra. "Just as I'd suspected. Come back at two o'clock sharp. We have a great deal to talk about."

Seven

WE DRIFTED OUT INTO THE HALL TOGETHER until we found ourselves at the elevator, and a moment later we were stepping inside. The elevator operator tipped his hat, then silently pushed the button. L was for lobby, I assumed.

Ah-choo!

"My name is Akiko," the mouth breather said in a voice like sandpaper. And she stuck her hand out first for me to shake, then for the overly polite girl. "Akiko Nakano. I'm allergic to dogs, along with just about everything else."

She let out another sneeze as we all shook hands, then adjusted a tortoiseshell barrette in her short black hair. I wasn't sure what to make of Akiko. With the war raging in the Pacific, meeting a Japanese kid trying out for a government job, well . . . Weren't we at war with them? I thought about my dad and his bomber plane and the battle reports on the radio.

My heart jumped to my throat.

I decided to fix my eyes on the arrow above the elevator door, which ticked off the floors we were passing. And I sneaked a glance at Akiko.

She was only an inch or so shorter than me and just as bony. Her orange skirt and blouse were faded and seemed a size too large. I figured that, like me, she was wearing hand-me-downs. She carried a canvas pouch printed with a comic book cover—*Hauntima, Mystery Woman of the Jungle*—at her hip, the wide strap slung diagonally across her chest. That was encouraging. Like me, she was interested in comic books. She pulled a hankie out of the bag and noisily began to blow her nose.

I watched her steady brown eyes studying me, from the cuffs of my wide-legged denim pants to the collar of my Gerda's Diner shirt. I might not have looked like a great puzzler either. But with the war on, I preferred to dress like the people I'd seen in the newsreels at the movie theater— like the land girls over in England. Now, those girls were helping fight the war, even if growing cucumbers and tending sheep didn't seem like much either.

"I'm Josephine O'Malley," I said. "But everybody calls me Josie."

"You sound a little like Winston Churchill," Akiko said. "Are you really a Brit? Or just pretending to be one?"

"Irish," I said, a little thrown off that she could hear an accent. I didn't know I had one. "We've lived in America since I was eight."

"I'm from San Francisco, but I don't think I have a California accent," Akiko said. "Best city in America, though I've only been to two others before now. Everybody like me was moved into camps, so I had to come live with cousins here in Philadelphia now."

I shoved my hands into my pockets and stared into Akiko's itchy allergy eyes. I'd heard what happened to the Japanese on the West Coast, but I didn't really understand it. Since Japan had bombed Pearl Harbor in Hawaii and started a war with us, President Roosevelt had everyone of Japanese blood who was living out West rounded up and locked up behind barbed wire in camps—whether they were American-born citizens or not.

I looked at her and imagined my dad and his plane taking fire from the Japanese gunners in the Pacific Ocean. What if they brought the fighting to San Francisco or Los Angeles or any of the cities out West?

I didn't know what to say, so I kicked my foot and avoided her gaze.

Thankfully, the curtsy dropper chimed in.

"I'm Mae Eugenia Crumpler of Chicago, Illinois," she said in a dignified sort of way that reminded me of charm school rather than puzzle solving. Then she shook my hand too in an awkward, formal sort of way. "Pleased to make your acquaintances. I don't know a thing about San Francisco, and I'm only visiting Philadelphia for the summer. But I do know puzzles. That's why I tried out for the job."

Akiko rubbed her itchy eyes, then began fumbling with the strap on her bag.

"I'm really good at figuring things out too," she said. "That's why I answered the ad." Akiko's voice dropped to almost a whisper. "My brother is fighting against the Nazis in Europe—he's in the 442nd. That's the army's all-Japanese regiment of soldiers. I just want to be like Tommy and do my part too."

My stomach flipped. And it wasn't just because the elevator came to a sudden stop as it reached the lobby. Like Akiko, I'd come here today to try for the puzzler job so that I could do something for the war.

Maybe this itchy asthmatic and I weren't that different after all.

"What do you know about Room Twelve?" I whispered as we stepped into the lobby. "What do you think that man—Mr. Hissler—was talking about?"

Akiko shrugged dramatically, but Mae ducked like she

didn't want anybody to notice us. "Room Twelve is pretty secret," she whispered, stepping closer to Akiko and me as we crossed the marble floor. "We shouldn't speak of it in the open like this."

"Then let's go someplace where we can talk without being overheard," croaked Akiko.

"Libraries are quiet places," offered Mae as we pushed through the Carson Building's fancy revolving door and out into the sunshine. "But I don't really want to go back to the library where my granny's working and have her shush us. I told Granny Crumpler I'd be gone all day, so I'm happy to find somewhere else to talk."

"Same," said Akiko, itching one eye. "My aunt and uncle's store is so busy. I'm not up for another day of stocking shelves."

"Let's go to the park," I said. "We can find a spot where nobody will overhear us but the squirrels."

So we set out together, Akiko, Mae, and I, walking a handful of blocks until we reached the iron gates that opened into Cosmo the Ultra Wizard Park. I looked around for a place where we could be alone, no distractions. Akiko and I sat down on a tree stump, eager to hear what Mae could tell us about this mysterious Room Twelve. I spied a pack of kids at the far end near a pond, but otherwise nobody was around to overhear us.

Mae began pacing back and forth, weaving her hands

together as she collected her thoughts. Her hair was black like Akiko's and curly like mine. But her curls seemed to have a strategy—rolls and loops in an organized pattern. My curls tended more toward chaos. Mae's eyes were dark brown and her skin even darker. I noticed her flowery purple skirt was ironed to perfection, and her shoes were polished bright like she was going to church. I wondered if everybody from Chicago dressed so nicely.

"I know that telling secrets is not polite," she began. "However, since you both were as insulted as I was by that Hank Hissler, I believe it's all right to share a bit."

"From the way Josie answered his question about her friend Emmett, I'd say she's not too worried about politeness," Akiko joked. And jabbing my ribs with her bony elbow, she issued a laugh that sounded like air escaping from a tire. Then she reached into her canvas pouch and pulled out a pair of sandals. Mae and I watched her kick off her black-and-white saddle shoes, then her socks, and tuck them into the bag before slipping into the sandals.

I couldn't help but wonder what else she carried around in that Hauntima pouch.

"Okay, let's get down to business. Can you tell us about Room Twelve?" I asked, eager to learn what I could. "Like where is it? On the first floor of the Carson Building? Or the seventh floor? And can we see what Mr. Hissler is up to if we sneak back over there? Spill it, already, will you?"

Mae stopped her pacing, then perched on the edge of a round rock across from where we were on the stump. She leaned in closer, so Akiko and I did too. Our three heads were nearly touching.

"You have to raise your right hands and take a vow of secrecy about Room Twelve," she said, "because this is top secret business. Granny Crumpler came across some classified documents at the library, and I took a peek."

I raised an eyebrow at her, not sure if I was ready to believe there actually was a real live "Granny Crumpler," let alone one who stumbled onto classified documents.

"Granny is a librarian," Mae said flatly, as if that explained everything. She blinked her long lashes a few times, waiting for Akiko and me to show our understanding. "Have you never met a librarian? They read the most surprising things."

Suddenly something caught my eye over Mae's shoulder. I saw movement on the path, and I leapt to my feet in alarm.

The kids I'd noticed at the pond along the far end of the park were approaching now, and I could see their gang leader: Toby Hunter. It came as no surprise to me that they were skipping school. I counted five of them pedaling bicycles, and the two smallest bullies were on shiny, candy-apple red ones—my brothers' bikes.

Anger sparked inside me. Those bikes had been a gift from our cousin Kay.

Kay's work at the neighborhood market helped Mam

take care of us. She gave a little from her paychecks to chip in on the rent and the groceries—just like I was doing with the money I earned working at Gerda's Diner. Only Kay made better money. And sometimes she did wonderful things for my brothers and me with it.

I couldn't bear to see these mean kids on my brothers' bikes—Kay's bikes.

"It's time to right a wrong." I gulped, stepping toward the approaching gang. "I'm not going to let the meanies win anymore."

"Meanies?" whispered Akiko to Mae. "Did she just say *meanies*? What is she, five years old?"

"Whatever you want to call them," I snapped, shooting Akiko a fierce look. She was one of those people whose whisper is almost exactly as loud as her regular speaking voice. "I am done letting mean people win. Those red bikes belong to my little brothers."

"I'm right beside you," said Mae, jumping to her feet. "I can't tell you the number of times I've had to deal with mean people."

Akiko stepped to the other side of me in a flash. "Count me in too. Somebody rode off on my bike before we even left San Francisco. I guess they thought because I was Japanese, stealing didn't count."

The three of us lined up along the path, blocking Toby and his band of bullies.

"What have we got here? A blockade? What do you want, Josie? To intimidate us?" His words stung like a smack on the cheek. "This is a joke, right? You're a bunch of fleas." Then he and his pals began laughing. It reminded me of noisy seagulls picking over garbage at the beach.

"By the way, Josie, there's something I've wanted to ask you about," Toby said, his eyes fixing on me with a steely coldness. "I saw the Western Union deliveryman going up the stairs to your apartment last week or so. Was he giving your mom a telegram?"

The sparks ignited now, turning into a full-blown fire.

"Don't you dare," I said, my voice barely above a whisper. "Don't you dare talk about my father. Not a word."

"Seems like you're keeping a secret—"

"I don't want to hear your insults, Toby," I snapped, talking over his horrible words. "I just want the bikes you stole from my brothers. Give them back."

"What're you talking about, Josie?" he asked in an innocent-sounding voice, a wicked grin spreading across his face. "We *found* these bikes, so they're ours fair and square. Now get out of our way or we'll pancake you."

"Like I said, I don't want a fuss." I grabbed the handlebars of what I knew was Vinnie's bike. "I just want what's fair. You took the bikes; now you need to give them back."

"Did your church's priest come with the telegram delivery?" said Toby, pushing me to the very brink of what I could take. "I thought I saw a white collar trailing behind the Western Union boy."

"Enough," I growled, yanking the handlebars.

Angry now, Toby shoved me back. I stumbled a few steps but caught myself. Without thinking twice, I dove for him, knocking him to the ground.

Suddenly Mae and Akiko were beside me, pulling my arms and shouting for me to stop fighting. But I was done playing nice. I could taste the gritty dust from the path. It mixed with the bitter words and flying elbows. Things were getting ugly, fast.

As Akiko and Mae pushed and pulled against Toby and the others, I grabbed the handlebars of Baby Lou's bike this time. But as I started to drag it to the side, one of Toby's bullies ripped it from my hands and sent me tumbling. He pedaled away with a noisy laugh, stirring up a cloud of dirt that made me choke.

Toby and the others knocked Akiko to the ground, and as Mae held on to Vinnie's handlebars, the boy now on that bike kicked at her. Mae stumbled onto the pathway, scraping one of her knees.

Cheering and chortling and pumping their fists in the air, Toby and his gang of goons sped off. I watched Vinnie's and Baby Lou's bikes disappear, a streak of candy-apple red cutting the horizon. I closed my eyes, hoping to keep the hot tears of frustration from burning my cheeks.

"Hauntima's ghost!" heaved Akiko, noisily catching her breath. "I can't believe what a bully that kid is! He kept those bikes! Your bikes! Josie, you must be so angry."

Mae helped me to my feet, even though her knee was bleeding. "You can't let it get the best of you, Josie. A kid like that, he's not worth it."

I stared off at the dust cloud, my hand reaching to my back pocket. At least they didn't take my Zenobia comic book.

"One of these days . . . ," I said, trying hard to keep my voice steady. Just as I'd done this morning when they'd first stolen the bikes, I wished somebody would come along and put a stop to bullies like Toby. "*One of these days* can't get here fast enough."

Eight

KIKO, MAE, AND I RINSED OUR KNEES and elbows in the nearby fountain. My hands were shaking as I cupped them, splashing water on my face. The thought of letting Vinnie and Baby Lou down twisted my stomach like a dish towel. And telling Cousin Kay and Mam that those beautiful red bikes were gone? My heart climbed into my throat.

I sat there quiet for a while.

"Forget about those mean kids," Mae said, wincing at her scraped knee as she perched at the edge of the water, the tall fountain spraying behind her. "Let's get over to Room Twelve. Mrs. Boudica said to come back this afternoon."

"And we need to find out more about that Mr. Hissler and what he's up to with the puzzler tryout," added Akiko. "Why would he want just the boys?"

"Maybe he doesn't think girls can solve puzzles," said Mae, wrinkling her forehead. "I can operate a cipher wheel. Can you?"

"Of course I can," Akiko said, pushing back a strand of her hair and giving Mae a confident look. "What kind of puzzler can't?"

"Before we get sidetracked proving our puzzling skills, go on, Mae," I urged. "You were about to tell us everything you know."

We had been in the middle of promising not to share these secrets with anybody. Sitting beside Mae on the fountain's marble rim, Akiko and I raised our right hands and began our pledge.

"I, state your name," Mae recited formally, as if she were swearing us in to the Supreme Court.

"I, Akiko Nakano."

"I, state your name," I repeated.

Mae stared at me, and Akiko smacked her hand to her face.

"Don't you know how an oath works?" Mae said gently, like I was three years old and needed the world explained to me. "When I say 'state your name,' you state your name."

Akiko's eyes peeked out from behind her fingers, and

I knew she was questioning my smarts. "She's a few colors short of a rainbow," I heard her mumble to Mae.

"Sorry," I said, cringing. I sat up straighter and rattled my head back and forth. If I wanted to keep up with Mae and Akiko, I'd better step it up. "I, Josephine Mary Maeve O'Malley."

Mae went on leading the pledge, her expression earnest and sweet.

"I do solemnly swear to keep the secrets I am about to hear and any others I might learn about henceforth, so help me Zenobia, Protector of Innocents!"

Akiko and I dropped our hands.

"Zenobia?" said Akiko, pulling a hankie from her canvas pouch and blowing her nose. "What about the other great superheroes? Like Hauntima? Or Hopscotch? Even Nova the Sunchaser?"

"Zenobia?" I asked too, jumping to my feet in excitement. "Are you talking about the superhero who used to fly over Philadelphia? *That* Zenobia?"

Mae nodded, her face lighting up like a Ferris wheel. "Zenobia saved the Liberty Bell from being stolen," she said, ticking off a list with her fingers, "after some supervillain tried to wreck parts of Independence Hall. Then she pushed the Statue of Liberty back onto her feet after another baddie knocked her over. And then—"

"Didn't President Roosevelt award the Medal of

Brave Deeds to Zenobia?" interrupted Akiko.

"Yes! Zenobia won it after she was injured in a battle called the Triple Threat—three villains, it happened in the third month of 1933," I said, my words tumbling out almost faster than I could form them. "President Roosevelt said he was awarding it because of her courage and selflessness in protecting so many innocent people when those bad guys tried to run that train off the tracks.

"There's even a big marble statue of her here in the city," I continued. "It's in the middle of a fountain in a park not far from . . ."

And suddenly all three of us turned our heads to gaze up at the carved stone figure looking down on us.

"Zenobia!" we shrieked, jumping together.

Standing right in the middle of the fountain and chiseled in white marble was the figure of a warrior, one arm raised as if in flight, the other cradling an orb—was that supposed to be Earth? Though her cape was made of stone too, it seemed to ripple gracefully behind her.

"That's the thing with superheroes these days," said Mae with a sad shake of her head. "Seems like they can only be found in statues and comic books. Not flying over cities and battling evil like they used to."

"You mean they're not in Chicago anymore either?" I asked. "Or San Francisco?"

Mae and Akiko shook their heads.

Where had all the superheroes gone? And why had they disappeared?

"It's easy to see why everyone loves Zenobia and her sister, the Palomino," Akiko said, wiping her nose. She tucked her hankie back into her pouch and pulled out a peppermint candy. Then she ran her fingers across the lettering that decorated the bag's front: HAUNTIMA. "But let's face it, Hauntima had the best powers of all. She could fly. She could make things levitate, read minds, control the weather, summon animals to fight for her."

"Sure, Hauntima was great and all." Mae shrugged. "But how could anybody fight crime in a nightgown? And barefoot? She needed a cape! And some boots!"

"And maybe a good mask like Hopscotch's," agreed Akiko. "When Hauntima's face transformed from human into that angry skull, it was a little creepy."

"Why do you talk about them in the past tense?" I asked, staring up at the stone Zenobia. "It's like you think they're gone forever. They can't be. I cannot believe heroes like Hauntima, Zenobia, and the Palomino would quit."

"Why wouldn't they?" asked Akiko. "When people keep making such a mess of things? There was too much for them to do, I guess. So they hung up their capes."

Mae's expression went soft. "Lots of people have lost hope. But I haven't. Sometimes I imagine I could be like them and have superpowers too. I want that more than anything—to fly to the front lines in France and make sure my daddy's okay. He's an ambulance driver in the war."

"I'd fly to my brother, Tommy," whispered Akiko. "Wherever he's fighting."

The three of us fell quiet. And I knew we were doing the same thing: thinking about the people we loved. And how this terrible war could take them from us forever.

Nine

"OKAY, ENOUGH WITH THE SUPERHEROES," Akiko said. "Tell us what you know about Room Twelve, Mae. And we promise to keep it to ourselves—just the three of us."

Mae stretched her neck and looked all around, making sure nobody was nearby listening. Then the three of us tucked in close together on the fountain's ledge, our foreheads touching this time.

Suddenly, as we pressed together, a surge of electricity pulsed through me. It wasn't as painful as when I touched a bedroom lamp after a shower when my feet were still wet. This sensation was strange, like a faint electrical current thrumming through my arms and legs.

Mae and Akiko must have felt it too, because they jumped backward at the same time I did. We looked at one another suspiciously.

"Okay, let's try that again," Mae began. We pressed in close again, this time with our shoulders forming a tight triangle. And again the crackling energy returned.

"Room Twelve is one of the most top secret programs in military history," Mae whispered. "Spies, secret codes, false identities, you name it. They've planted undercover operatives all over the world."

My eyes bugged wide enough to roll right out of my head like a couple of marbles.

"What does this have to do with puzzles?" Akiko asked with a noisy sniffle. "The advertisement that brought us to the Carson Building talked about 'math minds' and 'cracking codes' and 'big brains.' None of the people trying out today looked like secret agents!"

Mae shook her head.

"That's the thing. Room Twelve is top secret. The operatives working for it look like ordinary people—they dance the jitterbug, sell comic books at the newsstands, even put curlers in their hair at night. Room Twelve wants everyone to believe they're ordinary. But in reality, they're something much, much bigger. They're *extra*ordinary."

My mind was thunderstruck.

"I work at the diner on Captain Flexor Street. You mean

Gerda or Harry, the people who flip the pancakes, maybe they could be secret agents? Or my cousin Kay McNulty from County Donegal in Ireland? You mean she could be doing secret work for the war effort?"

Suddenly a thought dropped like an ice cube down the back of my shirt. Why hadn't I thought more seriously about this before? Mam told me and my little brothers that Cousin Kay worked as a cashier at Caruso's Market, ringing up sales of apples and milk and all that. I saw her leave for work every day with my own eyes: Kay slipping on her nice jacket, Kay tugging her red hat over her hair, Kay carrying a matching red pocketbook.

Was it possible she was doing something different? Something secret? Questions snagged at the edges of my mind, the way a hangnail catches fabric.

Didn't most grocery stores close at seven o'clock? Why was Kay sometimes working past midnight and through to morning? Why, if her job was to ring up sales of things as basic as salted crackers, did I sometimes see Kay at the kitchen table using a slide rule and working through complicated geometry problems? And why, if she was a simple cashier at a grocery store, was Kay reading library books about ballistics, bombs, and guns?

Suddenly Room Twelve didn't sound so far-fetched.

"From what I hear, Room Twelve tries to catch bad guys everywhere," Mae went on. "There are people all over the country spilling secrets to the Germans and the Japanese. . . ."

Mae's words snapped me back: *the Germans and the Japanese.* And like a newsreel at the Saturday matinee, images of planes crashing, bombs dropping, and enemy guns firing at our troops played in my mind. My heart leapt high in my throat, and I squeezed my eyes shut. My father.

Ah-choo!

Akiko wiped her nose, then fiddled with her hankie. When she looked up in the heavy silence that had fallen between us, I could tell she was trying to figure out our expressions. She glanced from my face to Mae's and back again.

"I've seen those looks before," she said, rubbing her irritated eyes. When she was done, they were pinker than ever, and she blinked rapidly to clear her vision and focus on the two of us again. I did the same thing whenever I was near my neighbor's cats. Their fur made my eyes so itchy, I could barely keep them open. "It was the same in San Francisco, when we had to leave home. You look at me, but you see the enemy."

I thought about Akiko's brother risking his life fighting for our side against the Nazis, even though his family was locked up behind barbed wire in an internment camp in California. And thoughts of my German friends at the diner, Gerda and Harry, leapt to my mind too. Gerda and

Harry being German didn't make them Nazis. Just because Akiko looked a lot like the enemy—the enemy that shot at my father in the Pacific—didn't mean she was the same as them, did it?

Mae and I watched Akiko blow her nose, then stuff the hankie back into her Hauntima bag. She looked at us again with her itchy, irritated eyes.

And it occurred to me that prejudices were a lot like allergies.

They made it hard for us to really see.

Ten

$\mathcal{S}$O, WHAT SHOULD WE DO ABOUT ROOM Twelve?" I asked, a little worried at the thought of having been so close to spies and undercover operatives. "It sounds like it could be dangerous."

"True, like that Hank Hissler," said Mae. "I didn't get a good feeling about him. Do you think Room Twelve is actually up to bad things?"

"I don't want to get into any kind of trouble," said Akiko.

I thought of my mom and all her worrying. Trouble was the last thing I needed too.

Stay safe, Mam was always warning me. *I can't bear it. . . .*

"We have until two o'clock to think about it," began Mae. "I say we—"

Suddenly Akiko gasped and shot her hands to her head, interrupting Mae.

"Dangerous or not, it doesn't matter! We've got to get back to Room Twelve. Now," she said, jumping to her feet and sending a few pebbles into the air. "I left my hat up in that place, and it's my auntie's favorite. She'll yell at me if I come home without it!"

We took off through the iron gates and back to the sidewalk, retracing our steps through downtown all the way to the Carson Building. Racing up the back staircase, it wasn't too hard to reach the seventh floor again and find those brass numbers reading ROOM 745. We knew the mysterious Room Twelve was somewhere nearby.

All three of us slipped inside, Akiko rushing around in search of her hat. Mae and I fanned out to explore the desks and peek into a few cabinets. I was looking for some sort of clue about spying, but I wasn't so sure what it might be. A telescope? A camera? A magnifying glass like Sherlock Holmes used?

But before any of us could explore further, a bark broke the silence. And suddenly a brown-and-white ball of fur raced over from the back of the room and jumped onto a steamer trunk that was serving as a coffee table for a sofa and chairs. Tail wagging wildly, he seemed happy to see us.

It was the same dog from this morning!

"Astra!" Mae shouted, throwing her arms around his furry neck. "I can't believe it's you. I met him for the first time last night at the library, just as Granny and I were closing up. He sat down right in front of the comic book display."

Akiko looked excited too, but she kept her distance. Probably worried about dog dander making her sneeze.

"So you met him before too? That's odd," she said, looking a little puzzled. "I ran into Astra early this morning, before the exam. He followed me on an errand I was running for my uncle's shop. Astra seems pretty smart . . . for a dog."

I couldn't believe this coincidence.

"And I met him this morning before I came here, when I was sweeping up in front of Gerda's Diner," I said, completely baffled. "The woman with him turned out to be . . ."

"Mrs. Boudica—" began Mae.

"She acted like she wasn't paying attention to what was happening around her," interrupted Akiko, "but I could tell she was. I saw her writing things down in a little notebook."

"That's right," came a confident voice from the back of the room. Mae jumped, and Akiko dropped her Hauntima bag. I stepped around Astra, nearly falling over. "I've been observing you girls—all three of you."

A brown leather chair spun slowly around, and Mrs. Boudica herself was sitting there. Her elbows rested on the chair's arms, and her fingertips pressed together like a pointy rooftop.

"While we spoke earlier, we haven't been formally introduced. I'm Constance Boudica. But please, call me Mrs. B," she said. "I have been observing the three of you for some time now. Though it's not just *I* who was observing, I should say, but *we*. And we like what we see.

"Room Twelve has taken a series of hits lately. And we're having to rethink our strategy. We've been looking for the right combinations of traits and skills. And you girls just might have them."

"Like what?" I wanted to know.

"Like determination, compassion, and perseverance.

"Like intelligence, heart, and spirit.

"Like justice, selflessness, and courage."

Ah-choo!

Akiko looked stricken. "Courage? Why in the world are you looking at me, then? Or her?" she added, hooking her thumb at Mae. "She wears socks with lace edges."

"I beg your pardon?" whispered Mae, clearly annoyed by Akiko's insult. "Leave my footwear choices out of this!"

"Or me," I said, my voice cracking. I took a moment to clear my throat. "I'm not exactly the most courageous person you'll ever find."

Mrs. B's eyes flicked to Mae's bloody knee. To my scuffed dungarees. And to Akiko's messy hair. Akiko unclipped her barrette; then she smoothed down a few stray clumps and clipped the barrette back in.

"We all must fight injustice however we can," Mrs. B said, getting to her feet. As she crossed the room toward us, I noticed she walked with a slight limp, her left leg seeming to move at an awkward angle. "And that is precisely what I'd like to speak with the three of you about. I've studied your exams for the puzzler tryout, and I am quite impressed with your abilities there. You see, Room Twelve involves clever thinking and attention to details.

"The three of you, I believe, offer promising hope."

Mrs. B was talking about the three of us like we were a team. But we'd met only this morning. And, to be perfectly honest, we couldn't be more different. And it wasn't just the color of our skin, the texture of our hair, or where our families came from. It was so much more—like how Mae wore dresses with pleats that were ironed stiff and straight. And she kept her hair rolled neat and tidy. Glancing over at Mae, I couldn't stop myself from running a hand over my own wild mop of curls, patting them into place.

And Akiko? She dressed in mismatched hand-me-downs and seemed to carry a general store in her canvas Hauntima bag. While Mae was charm-school prim and polished, Akiko was messy: a mouth breather who interrupted people whenever they were speaking.

I figured I must fall somewhere in between. I pulled my comic book from my back pocket and rolled it up in my hands like a tube.

Astra circled Mrs. B's feet, then hopped back onto the brown steamer trunk and sat down. He gazed at us with watchful eyes as Mrs. B went on.

"We've never seen three girls who were more alike."

I heard Mae issue a little gasp and Akiko cough. I rattled my head to pay closer attention.

"Each one's strength seems to complement the others'. And then there's the obvious:

"All three of you appear obsessed with superheroes.

"All three of you go to bed at night worried about someone you love.

"And all three of you want—more than anything—to do whatever you possibly can to keep them safe."

This Mrs. B was smarter than I'd first thought.

"I believe I have what you're looking for, Miss Nakano, do I not?" she asked, holding a straw hat out before her. Astra took it from her hand and padded over to Akiko, who accepted it from the dog's jaws with a look of complete disgust. Akiko held it up with a single finger, so the least amount of canine contamination would touch her.

"Thanks," she said, without the slightest enthusiasm. "Good, um, little doggy."

Astra sat down at Akiko's feet, one ear raised curiously, as if studying her.

Then a sound on the other side of the closed door caught his attention. Suddenly Astra bounded to the doorway and began barking frantically. Mrs. B rushed over and swung it open. In an instant, she and Astra crossed the hallway and into the next room.

So of course Mae, Akiko, and I followed.

I couldn't believe the commotion as we stepped inside. There seemed to be a fight going on. A man in a dark suit and a gray fedora hat was yelling at another figure, who wore all black. Only this second man wasn't in a traditional business suit like the first. He was wearing a costume—a long black cape, a black mask, and tall black boots.

A caped hero? I couldn't believe my eyes! It had been so long!

"What are you playing at, Hissler?" hollered the man in black. "I don't trust your motives! Come back here and explain yourself!"

Mrs. B and Astra had rushed toward them too. "Mr. Hissler, I've asked you before, what do you think you're—"

Hank Hissler didn't explain himself. Instead he barreled past them toward the door. Akiko, Mae, and I stumbled out of his way just in time, but my comic book slipped from my hands onto the floor.

The man in the black cape—it must have been the

Stretcher, a legendary superhero whom my dad had admired when he was a boy—reached out to grab Mr. Hissler. His long black arm stretched nearly the whole length of the room!

Just as the Stretcher caught hold of Mr. Hissler's suit collar, the room erupted in a burst of white light. It blinded my eyes. And the crack that accompanied it sounded like shattering glass.

In the frantic seconds that followed, blinking and waving away the smoke, I realized that both Mr. Hissler and the Stretcher were gone. I heard pounding footsteps and a sinister cackle, which told me our snake-eyed instructor was escaping down the hall. But what about the Stretcher?

Once the smoke thinned out, I saw where Akiko and Mae were staring. Following their gaze down to the floor, to where he had been standing only seconds before, I noticed a few sparks sizzling into the smoky air. All that remained of the Stretcher was a pair of black boots, a shimmery black cape, and a black mask.

Coughing and wheezing, Mrs. B, Akiko, Mae, and I fanned the air and tried to make sense of the scene. Astra barked and raced to the door and back a few times.

I reached down and gently picked up the cape, surprised by its heft. The fabric looked light and airy, but it weighed more than I'd expected. Beside me, Mae squatted to the floor and collected the two boots. Akiko scooped up the mask and turned it around delicately in her hands.

"This," said Mrs. B breathlessly, trying to control her anger. "This is what we're up against. A force darker than any of us could have imagined. With each attack, another caped hero disappears. Vaporized. There have been far too many taken from us to count."

"That's not fair," I said, trying not to yell. "Vaporizing superheroes? Eliminating those who are trying to do good in the world?"

"Who?" fumed Mae. "Who would do such a thing?"

"And how can they be stopped?" wheezed Akiko, her cheeks as pink as her irritated eyes.

Mrs. B turned to face the three of us, and her expression was fierce.

"This is where you come in," she began. "We think you can help. Room Twelve would like you to join in solving this, our biggest puzzle.

"As I've said before, our league of secret heroes sees something in each one of you. And even more important, we see the potential of what the three of you bring together."

I was about to ask a question when a shout from the hall interrupted us.

"Mrs. B! Come quick!" A man staggered into the doorway and leaned against the frame, panting for air. "The maps room caught fire. It's spreading fast!"

Astra and Mrs. B raced out the door, leaving Akiko,

Mae, and me to stare at one another in the silence.

"We've got to help," Akiko said in her sandpaper voice. "But how?"

"Can't we chase after them?" said Mae, eagerly turning toward the door, the black boots in her arms. "If people are in danger, we've got to do something."

I wanted a moment to think. So I reached over and clutched Mae's shoulder, hoping she'd wait before running off.

As my hand touched Mae, sparks suddenly crackled in the air above our heads, and a small jolt of electricity pulsed through my arms and body. Mae jumped. She grabbed Akiko's hand in surprise, her eyes wide. And again, sparks sizzled into the air.

"What'd you do that for?" Akiko gasped, clutching the black mask to her chest in surprise. "You shocked me!"

"I didn't mean to," Mae said. "It's coming from these boots, I think. What's happening in here?"

I couldn't make sense of the electricity in the room. It hummed in my ears. And the cape I was holding in my hands seemed to shudder with energy.

"If only we had powers like Hauntima," said Akiko, "then we'd know exactly how to help those people down the hall." The pulsing electrical current now seemed to kick up a notch.

"That's it!" I whispered. "Maybe we can."

I stepped close to the both of them, throwing the black cape over my shoulders and fastening it at my neck. As I did, the thrumming in my ears surged even louder. "Do the same," I urged them, gesturing at the costumes in their hands. Akiko slipped the mask over her eyes, and Mae kicked her shoes off and swiftly tugged on the boots. Now a fountain of sparks shot into the air above us.

As Mae, Akiko, and I pressed in closer together, throwing our arms around one another's shoulders, the room suddenly filled with a yellow glow. The thrumming sound grew stronger until it became a dizzying pounding in my ears, and we leaned in close not only so we could hear one another but also for encouragement. My voice shook as I tried to speak.

"Th-there must be power left over in the Stretcher's costume," I stammered. "In the c-cape, mask, and boots."

"Power to do what?" shouted Mae. "What happens now?"

"Power to transform into superheroes, I hope!" hollered Akiko with a wild grin. "But we have to say something or do something to activate it!"

"What can it be?" I called over the pounding in my ears, my heart revving like a car's engine. I was frantic now. "What turns somebody into a superhero?"

"A gamma ray!" shouted Mae. "I read about that with Nova the Sunchaser! She was struck by a blast of electrons!"

"No, no, no," argued Akiko. "It's a radioactive potion. We have to find the recipe that will transform us from mere mortals into superpowered heroes!"

I shook my head. It couldn't be rays or potions. It had to be something right here, right now, within the tight triangle we'd formed with our shoulders.

"Grab my hand," I called over the pulsing in my ears. And I slipped my right arm into the center of our triangle. Mae and Akiko did the same. As the three of us grabbed hands, still clutching on to one another's shoulders, it finally came to me.

"We have to speak it!" I hollered. "Something sacred or important."

"That's too easy," complained Akiko. "Do you think maybe we need to be stung by an exotic bug? Like a scorpion or a giant wasp?"

"It should be an incantation," urged Mae. "Like the first letters of our favorite heroes' names!"

Zenobia, Palomino, and Hauntima? "You mean something like Ze-Pa-Ha? Or Ha-Pa-Ze?" I asked impatiently. "What about Hopscotch? And Nova the Sunchaser? Should we add them, too?"

We looked frantically into one another's faces.

"We've got to come up with something," Akiko hollered, "because all I want to do is help those innocent people down the hall."

"Right! And catch bad guys like that Mr. Hissler, after what he did to the Stretcher!" added Mae, agreeing with Akiko for what might have been the first time.

Helping innocent people. Catching bad guys.

My thoughts raced to my little brothers, so scared of meanies like Toby Hunter and his bullies. To my mom working two jobs, trying to keep our family safe from any more harm. And to my dad flying planes in the war. I wanted to help them all.

My stomach turned somersaults. Taking a deep breath, I whispered into the triangle, "I want a chance to do some good."

Suddenly a beam of golden light burst from the center of our huddle, radiating upward from our connected hands. The walls around us lifted, then dropped with a jolt. And the air hummed like it was filled with a thousand bumblebees.

"What's happening?" gasped Mae, trying to steady herself in the blinding glow.

"Earthquake," Akiko announced sensibly, her eyes blinking rapidly under her mask. And as a wind kicked up and began to swirl around us, her hair whipped in all directions. "Earthquakes happen all the time in San Francisco."

"But we're not in San Francisco," I shouted, clinging tightly to our clasped hands. "We're here, in the Carson Building, wishing we had superpowers!"

The crackling electrical charge exploded in my ears

now, and energy shot through my veins. It was as if we were standing in the center of a hurricane. Light and wind spiraled around us, and the powerful pulsing surged through our fingers, arms, legs—our entire bodies. It lifted my feet off the floor, and the three of us seemed to levitate as the world just beyond us swirled around and around.

"Mae!" shouted Akiko in surprise. "You're turning purple!"

"And, Josie!" hollered Mae, her eyes wide. "Look at you!"

Streams of purple, orange, and green rippled in the funnel cloud as we hung there suspended in the pull and whoosh of the spiraling light. The wind whipped my hair, but as I looked down, I was able to catch sight of my tingling toes and feet.

They seemed to be turning green!

*W*ITH MAE AND AKIKO'S HELP, I WAS ABLE
to carry the trunk and the fire survivors down to safety
in the building's back garden. Not in the same trip, of
course, but it went quickly enough. I did take my time,
not because they were particularly heavy, but just so I
didn't slip down the stairs and make a fool of myself.
My knees were shaking and my mind was reeling—not
only from our newfound powers, but also from seeing
Hauntima's ghost. On my last run, as I was carrying one
of the grown-ups, Mae climbed down right behind me.
Her own arms were loaded with Astra on one side and

another weak and weary fire victim on the other.

"She's starting to come to," Mae said, a little breathless. "I can't believe it! I saved her life!"

Once we reached the bottom, an office manager saw Mae and let out a tearful cry of relief. "Thank you, thank you," he sighed, scooping the soot-covered, overweight cat from Mae's arms. "Mrs. Tubbytons is my best friend!"

"It's funny," Mae said, reluctantly handing over the rescued tabby. "She seems more Queen Anastasia than Mrs. Tubbytons."

"Oh, brother," complained Akiko, rolling her eyes behind her orange mask. "Nobody is going to take us seriously now."

I stared around the Carson Building's garden at the chaos. Sirens from the steady stream of fire trucks pierced the air, and the evacuated office workers were tromping over rosebushes and yellow pansies. Some of the workers I'd seen already up on the seventh floor—were they part of Room Twelve? Others were unfamiliar and probably worked in offices throughout the building.

Mae set Astra on the ground, and within moments Mrs. B appeared right behind him. Ashes stained her tailored dress and shoes, but she looked unshaken. "Well done, girls," she said coolly.

I saw her eyeing the steamer trunk before turning her full attention to the three of us.

"There is so very much to inform you about," she said quietly as the noise pressed in. It was as if she were trying to draw as little attention to our exchange as possible. I had to strain to hear her. "Thanks to your remarkable efforts on the seventh floor, everyone involved in our affairs is accounted for." Then she let out a heavy sigh. "Everyone, that is, except for one: Hank Hissler.

"We have no idea where he has disappeared to. But we know for sure he has betrayed us."

Images flashed through my mind—of the Stretcher moments before he was vaporized, of Mr. Hissler's snake-like eyes, of the devastating fire. My stomach lurched at the thought of Mr. Hissler asking me about Emmett. Thank goodness I hadn't revealed where to find him!

Camera bulbs flashed, lighting up the garden as news-paper photographers rushed over. I grabbed Akiko and Mae and nodded toward the iron gate that led to the street, giving them both my best we've-got-to-get-out-of-here look. The last thing I needed was for my mom or Kay to see a photograph of me running around Philadelphia in a funny costume, when I was supposed to be at school learning important things or at the diner earning rent money.

Thankfully, Akiko and Mae felt the same way. "If Granny sees me like this, I'll be in big trouble! Granny doesn't like people trying to be the center of attention."

"Oh no!" added Akiko. "I cannot have my picture in the paper! It's bad enough that I skipped a day helping in my uncle's store!"

But it was too late. Suddenly a reporter buzzed in front of my face, notepad open. "Who are you kiddies?" he said. "The Caped Curiosities? The Gallant Gals? Tell us your names, would ya?"

"Is this an early Halloween stunt?" called another journalist, scratching his ear with his pencil. "Are you dressed up for play? Will you show us the hidden wires that helped you carry those big lugs to safety?"

"Philadelphia hasn't seen caped heroes in years," said a third reporter. "Not since that Zenobia and her sister . . . What was she called—the Palomino? I remember when they knocked out the Stink back in 1939. Boy, that was an ugly battle. Those were some amazing superwomen."

"I could swear I saw Hauntima around here earlier," said the first reporter, looking a little perplexed. "But maybe it was a trick of the light with all that smoke. These kids are for real, though. Mighty Mites, that's who they are!"

Now a bigger crowd began pushing over to us, hollering questions and reaching out hands to touch our capes. The route to the iron gate was cut off, and I couldn't see another exit from the courtyard.

"Should we run back into the building?" said Mae, her voice tight. "They're getting closer."

"We could climb the fire escape again," said Akiko, pointing at the black stairs hanging off the side of the building. "Oh, never mind! There's a photographer on it now!"

Another camera bulb flashed, blinding us for a moment. We had to act fast to get away from this crowd, before an office manager grabbed us or the reporters jotted down too many details about who we were and where we lived. If there's one thing I knew from all my comic books, it's that superheroes needed to keep their real identities secret!

I made a break through the crowd and took off running for the courtyard's center, where a circle of benches faced one another. As I leapt over the low hedge surrounding it, I stumbled. But instead of falling down, I felt myself falling up. Like I was floating for a moment or two.

Like I was flying!

I could hear Akiko and Mae not far behind me.

"The only way out is up," I called over my shoulder, cape fluttering. "We've got to try!"

But as I leapt into the air again, hoping to take off, I caught my foot on a potted plant and tumbled onto the stone courtyard. The crowd behind us let out a groan. It must have looked pretty bad.

"What are you kids up to in those costumes? Did you have something to do with that fire?" called a police officer, waving his billy club in our general direction. "Take off the masks."

A second officer yelled even louder. "Are they with the circus?"

"I told you everybody'd think we were circus perfor—"

"Not now," I shouted to Akiko. "Leap!"

Back on my feet, I took off running again. Reaching my arms before me, I squinted my eyes tight and dove the way I did in the summertime at the swimming pool. But instead of arcing downward and splashing into water, my body seemed to lift up and back. The breeze on my cheeks felt cool despite the summer heat, and my emerald cape seemed to catch the wind.

I was flying!

Rising!

Soaring!

When I opened my eyes, the courtyard and the chaos were falling away. The trees and benches looked smaller, and the noise started to recede. Then Mae's friendly voice cut through the murmuring crowd.

She was still on the ground!

"You see, it's like this," she was explaining, probably to a police officer or another newspaper reporter. "We three kids had no idea—"

But just then the crowd erupted in shouts and whoops. I dared to glance behind me, and that's when I caught sight of Akiko shooting through the air. Her orange cape shimmered in the sunlight like a meteor's tail. Together we circled above the roof until we spied Mae rising too.

"We're flying!" shrieked Mae, who looked like a shimmery purple bird over the treetops. "We've got powers like Hauntima. Only with better costuming!"

We did a few more loops around the building, unable to pull ourselves away from the excitement. And we were slowly getting the hang of our newest superskill. Bright red fire trucks sat in the street, looking like toys from our view up so high. The police officers and the reporters in the courtyard shouted at us to come down, but there was no going back now.

I heard Astra barking and saw Constance Boudica gazing up at us. She had a smile on her face, and I could swear she gave us a small salute.

"Who are those kids?" shouted another voice from the crowd as we crested the Carson Building's roof. "What are they called?"

"I think that one in the purple said it," came another in reply. "'Wee Three' is what it sounded like."

"They're remarkable," said a third voice. "But that's a terrible name."

Thirteen

WE FLEW IN STUNNED SILENCE FOR A WHILE until we spotted a wide rooftop below us. I signaled to Mae and Akiko that we should land, and with a few shouts and tumbles, we came to a stop without killing ourselves or one another—though Akiko gave a flock of pigeons a good scare. I said something about our job being finished, and suddenly we transformed again. Only this time there was no golden light or wind. Our costumes suddenly morphed back into our regular clothes, right before our eyes.

And minutes after that, we were stepping onto the sidewalk as if nothing out of the ordinary had just happened.

"I . . . ," began Mae, her mouth moving like a fish's, silent and round. "I just . . ."

She couldn't find the words.

Neither could I. Nor Akiko, it seemed.

Threading past the late-afternoon commuters, we were too stunned, too shocked, too utterly *flabbergasted* to even speak. Since we'd overshot my neighborhood by a few miles, we would have to make our long, winding way through an unfamiliar part of the city. We set off in silence and let our minds turn the day's events around and around.

Finally, as we stood waiting for a traffic light to change on a busy street corner, Akiko spun and faced Mae and me. She fidgeted with the strap of her canvas bag. "So, what was she flying off to do?" she said, starting her question midthought. She just assumed we'd understand right away that she was referring to Hauntima. "One minute we were standing there, ordinary kids—well, *two* ordinary. One is a little odd—"

"What?" Mae exclaimed. "Who are you calling odd? Certainly not me!"

Akiko rolled her eyes and pressed on.

"I just don't get it," she said with an exaggerated shrug. "How did she know about the fire? Where did she come from? Why was she a ghost and not the real Hauntima?"

"And why . . . , " Mae added with a long pause. Her

expression was one of baffled awe as she gazed at Akiko and me. "Why us?"

We walked on down the sidewalk and past a small park. I was asking the same questions. In fact, I'd started to wonder whether the past few hours had even happened at all. Was I dreaming? Superheroes hadn't been seen in Philadelphia for so many years. What made today special? What made the three of us special? Sure, Mrs. B tried to explain it. But really? Did she *really* believe the three of us could make good superheroes?

My stomach began to growl, so I steered us toward a nearby diner whose sign blinked like a lighthouse. I set my course straight for it.

"I can't think clearly until I eat," I said. "I want to make sense of Astra, Mrs. B, Hauntima. Even the three of us. We saved people's lives today! All of this is such a mystery."

"Oh, how I love mysteries." Mae grinned, clasping at her heart. "Isn't it curious how we all had different powers, except for flying? And how that woman from the seventh floor looked so much like Mrs. Roosevelt? My granny met the first lady at an art center in Chicago. Granny said she is truly a lady and that one time—"

"What does that even mean?" interrupted Akiko, her sandpaper voice cracking. "*Truly a lady*? Does it mean she dabbed her lips with her napkin after each cookie? That she said *please* and *thank you* in all the right places?"

"To start with, she didn't interrupt," Mae replied, a few clouds passing across her usually sunny face.

I was too hungry to deal with Mae and Akiko and their bickering. They were starting to sound like my knuckle-head little brothers. And my stomach was protesting that we'd missed lunchtime, so I was getting crankier by the second. I stared hungrily at the bright neon sign that blinked my all-time favorite word in the English language: PIE.

"Let's talk about it over something to eat," I said, pulling open the diner's door and ushering the two of them toward the nearest booth. While Akiko and Mae kept at their squabble, I breathed in the aroma of fresh-baked blueberry pie. My mouth watered as I imagined that first bite.

"No, no, no, kiddos," said a burly manager, fanning a stack of menus at us like we were a bad smell. "Out you go."

"We'd just like some pie, please," I began, feeling the eyes of the patrons around us watching. I knew my cheeks were pink with embarrassment, and I wished we could just slip silently into the booth and not be the focus of such a fuss. "I have money to pay you," I whispered.

Did we look too scruffy to afford a meal? Sure, we probably smelled like a campfire, and I imagined our hair was a little tousled from the day's adventures. I peeked at Akiko and Mae, and they looked respectable enough. I ran a hand over my long curls, tamping down here and there where I could feel them poking out.

"Your money's no good here," the manager said gruffly, waving those menus at us again. "Now scoot. Scram. Beat it!"

Mae shot toward the door like a bottle rocket. Akiko followed behind her, though her gait was stiff and slow. But I didn't understand. I stayed put. Between my growling stomach and the delicious-looking desserts I'd spied on the long counter, I wasn't ready to walk out.

"Why won't you let us stay?" I gestured at the empty tables throughout the diner and the customers sitting here and there on either side of us. "There are plenty of seats. Nobody else is waiting. And you serve exactly what we're here to eat—pie."

The manager folded his meaty arms across his chest and shook his head. "Sure, kid, we serve excellent pie. But what we don't serve here is their kind. Now, goodbye."

I stumbled back out onto the sidewalk with Mae and Akiko, hot with anger. Why did he think it was okay to treat us that way? When all we wanted was a place to sit down and talk? I looked over at Mae, whose expression was hard as stone. Akiko's too. Any outrage I was feeling must have been multiplied a hundred times for them.

"I can't believe this," I said, my hands shaking. "He was so unfair. I didn't know people could act like—"

"Well, they can," Akiko seethed. "And they do."

Mae didn't speak. But I could see her chest heave as she took a breath.

I scratched my arm, not sure what to do with myself. In the bright sunshine, my freckles stood out on the pale skin at my wrists. Even though I was always complaining about it, this sunburn-prone skin let me go places my new friends couldn't. I peeked over at Mae again, and in my mind I pictured her trying to get pie with her daddy once he was back from the war. And I cringed just imagining another diner turning them away. How was this fair? Mae's dad and Akiko's brother could risk their lives—risk bullets and bombs defending our country in the war—but they couldn't sit down in some restaurants for a slice of pie?

As we set off walking, Akiko and Mae were quiet.

"It's like there're two wars," I said softly, glancing at the manager through the diner window. "One fighting against the Nazis and the other against people like him." I turned to face them both. "I'm so sorry."

Fourteen

"WHAT ARE YOU DOING BACK HERE, *Schätzchen?*" called Gerda from the kitchen as we walked into her diner. She and Harry were always giving me pet names like "honey" and "sweetheart." And they taught me lots of other German words too. "I thought you were going off to solve the puzzles!"

I blinked a moment or two. Even if I could tell them about my day, they wouldn't believe it. I hardly did myself.

"The tryout?" I said. "It didn't exactly work out."

"There'll be other opportunities, pal," said Harry. "Don't you worry."

I spotted an empty booth along the front windows, so

I dove into the seat on one side and signaled for Mae and Akiko to join me. They took their seats stiffly on the other side of the booth, their faces tense as they seemed to brace for another terrible insult from a manager.

"That's a shame, Josie," said Gerda in her thick accent, pouring more coffee for the regular customers at the tables beside us. "You're a hard worker. And so good with the words and the numbers. They made a mistake passing on you, *Schätzchen*. How about I bring you something to eat? You want the usual? Blueberry pie and a brown cow?"

In the year or so that I'd been working at Gerda's Diner, I had never ever changed my order. Gerda and Harry gave up trying to get me to eat something different ages ago.

"Thanks. Only this time with three forks and three straws, please," I said, pointing across the table. "My friends Akiko and Mae here, they got cut from the puzzler tryout just like me."

"It's okay, *Schätzchen*," Gerda said, consoling me with a gentle pat on the arm. And with a friendly nod to Akiko and Mae, she added, "Theirs is on the house too. You'll work it off tomorrow. What'll it be, girls?"

Mae was all manners and polite thank-yous, but Akiko started bouncing in her seat like it was Christmas morning. She ordered an egg cream and a slice of apple pie.

"And I'll have a chocolate malted, please," Mae said,

her hands folded neatly over her menu. "And if you have cherry pie, that would be lovely."

"We do," Gerda replied with a wink. "And it's very lovely."

We settled in talking, and before long Harry appeared with our milkshakes and a plate stacked with waffles. After introductions all around, he set everything down with a flourish. "We had an extra stack today," he announced, pulling a bottle of warm maple syrup from his apron pocket. Then, with a bow, he moved on to the table across from us to visit with some of the regulars. I pointed out Harry's friends to Akiko and Mae, and how everybody called the noisiest one by his nickname—"the Duke."

"The people here are so nice," whispered Mae, as if she were sitting at a table in a library instead of at a red leather booth in a busy diner. "How come they let you work here? When you're just a child, I mean."

"Same reason they let anybody work anywhere these days," I answered, trying hard not to slurp my brown cow. I knew slurping wouldn't go over so great with well-mannered Mae. Or her granny. So I wiped at my lips and tried to remember to swallow my chocolate drink before launching into my response. "Most all the men are off fighting the war. So who's going to clear the tables and wash the dishes? Gerda was desperate for help before I showed up."

"Do you need any more help?" wondered Akiko, just as

Gerda arrived with our pie slices. The warm, fruity smells were like heaven. "Since I can't be a puzzler, maybe I can be a pie server!" Gerda laughed and promised to keep Akiko in mind.

We started in on our pies and went over our day one more time. "First there's this morning," began Mae with a shudder, "and that awful Hank Hissler in the fedora—"

"He made me think of a snake," Akiko cut in, poking the straw around her drink. "Like there was something dangerous about him."

"I wonder why he asked about your friend Emmett," Mae said. "What do you think he's up to?"

"Well," I said, taking my time, "Emmett is really smart. He's probably the cleverest person I've ever met, besides my cousin Kay. He'd make a great puzzler."

"I worry that we could be getting ourselves tangled up in some dangerous things," said Mae, her expression pained. "Think about the Stretcher." And lowering her voice, she whispered, "What does it even mean to be vaporized?"

Akiko stopped her fork midbite. I pushed my drink away.

A wave of guilt washed over me. What would my mom think if she knew about all the risks I'd taken today? The only thing she'd asked of me was to stay out of trouble, to be safe, to take care of my brothers. I swallowed hard. There were rules about superheroes keeping their identities secret. Maybe that was because they all had mothers who worried as much as mine.

Akiko looked around the diner, and when she spoke, her voice was somber.

"If we're going to help people like we did today as super-heroes, we'll have to pay closer attention to what's going on around us. Hauntima watches out for all sorts of things in her comic books—villains, thieves, even crashing meteors."

I took an especially big bite of pie and looked out the window into the blue summer sky. No meteors that I could see. I thought for a bit as I chewed.

"Emmett is really good at that—noticing important things in what seems like the everyday, ordinary stuff," I told them. "One time he wrote me a secret message in laundry!"

Akiko and Mae said they didn't believe me.

"Honest! It was washing day, and he told his mom he would hang the wet clothes out to dry on the clothesline that was tied on their balcony. They lived on the second floor of their building, and I could see their back porch from the sidewalk. So Emmett hung this from left to right:

"Dress.

"Raincoat.

"Pants.

"Evening gown.

"Pajamas.

"Purse.

"Earmuffs—"

"Earmuffs?" interrupted Akiko. "That's not something you hang out to dry on your wash line!"

"Neither is a purse, smarty-pants," I continued, ignoring her constant interruptions. I thought for a moment, then remembered the last item:

"Robe."

Akiko and Mae looked perplexed. I couldn't tell whether they were trying to figure out Emmett's coded message or if they thought Emmett and I sounded crazy. I went on before I lost them.

"'What's my favorite soda pop?' That's what Emmett asked me on the sidewalk. When I said I thought it was Coca-Cola, he shook his head and told me the answer was staring me straight in the face. I looked for clues everywhere—in wrappers lying on the ground, in his eyes in case he was blinking a coded signal at me, in a nearby tree in case he'd slipped a note there the way spies did in my comic books. Finally he just laughed and told me to read his laundry line!"

"P-E-P-P-E-R?" asked Mae. "I thought maybe each of those items began with the letters that spelled out—"

"Dr Pepper!" shouted Akiko. And she was pointing excitedly at a Dr Pepper sign that hung on the wall above the soda fountain. "That's really clever. But also a little weird. Didn't you guys have better things to do?"

I laughed, and Mae did too. Akiko certainly could be annoying, with the nonstop interrupting and the way she was always practically wheezing. But Akiko was quick and smart, and when she spoke, you knew you were going to hear the honest-to-goodness truth. While I liked Mae's gentleness, I appreciated how Akiko was so direct.

I shoveled another bite of blueberry pie into my mouth and glanced over at Harry at the table beside us. His face was tense, and he didn't look at all happy. It made me wonder what he saw in his friends—the Duke and those other thick-necked men. They reminded me of Toby's gang of mean kids. Did Harry's friends make him laugh? Did they make him want to be a better person?

Emmett did that for me. And now maybe Akiko and Mae would too.

I stretched my ear into the aisle, trying to pick up on what Harry's table was talking about so secretively. Was it about the best baseball players? Or horse racing? Where to get a bargain on suits? Or were they talking about politics and the war?

And that's when I caught it—just a single word. But it burst in the air between us like a firecracker.

Spion.

I coughed, choking noisily on my pie crust. Because I knew exactly what that word meant in English:

Spy!

Fifteen

$\mathcal{M}$Y BODY WENT RIGID. I KEPT MY FACE
pointed at Mae and Akiko across the table from me, and
I moved my jaw in a steady motion, like I was focused on
chewing that delicious dessert. But I was so absorbed in
Harry and his friends' table that I could have fallen out of
my seat and into the aisle. I allowed only my eyes to move.
And they stared over at the loudest of Harry's friends, the
Duke, as if seeing him for the first time.

The Duke was old—maybe in his sixties. His eyes were
pale blue, and his wavy hair was always slicked back with
an oil of some sort. He was nice enough to me, though we
didn't laugh and talk the way Harry and I did. Harry let

me walk his dog and showed me photographs of his mother back in Germany, whom he missed so much. Harry and Gerda taught me German songs and German words, too, like *Schätzchen*, which meant "sweetie," and *stinkend*, which meant "smelly." And they fed me delicious German food like bratwurst and sauerkraut and spaetzle.

Spion.

The Duke said it again, more forcefully this time. And I watched him push something on the table for the other men to read. I looked all around for Harry, but he wasn't there among them now. Scanning across the restaurant, I caught sight of him walking back to his usual spot at the stove to flip pancakes again.

I had to turn my head an inch or so to catch what the Duke was doing. His usually boisterous voice was hushed now, and the others seated around his table leaned in close to examine the document. Their expressions were serious as they nodded, a few letting out *hmph* and *tsk-tsk* sounds as they followed along with the Duke's quiet directions.

As I stretched even farther toward the table now to hear, I practically fell out of the booth. Suddenly the Duke turned his meaty head and looked my way. My heart seemed to stop beating. Did the Duke know I was eavesdropping? That I understood a few German words? Was he going to come after me?

He put the cap on his pen, then pushed his chair back

and got to his feet, saying something to the four or five others in rapid German that I couldn't understand. Then the Duke rushed out of the diner without so much as a goodbye to Gerda or Harry.

"Flying is the best superpower of all," Mae was saying as she delicately nibbled another bite of her cherry pie. "You can say all you want about invisibility or X-ray vision—"

"Seriously? What about my power, shape-shifting? Or—" Akiko's sandpaper voice was growing louder with outrage. Her thoughts seemed to come too quickly for her to wait her turn in a conversation. Sometimes she even wound up interrupting herself. "You can call storms, Mae! Isn't *atmo-kinesis* better than flying?"

One by one, the other men rose and left the diner. "It's already five o'clock," I heard one of them say to his buddy as he ran a comb through his slick curls. "I've got to swing by for a haircut before that barber closes for the day."

"You should stop thinking so much about your hair and more about your neck," warned the other, running a thick finger across his throat like a knife.

And then they were gone. Slowly, I stepped over to their empty table and peered past the coffee mugs and plates of toast, hoping to catch sight of whatever it was the Duke had shown the others—a map or blueprints, maybe a list of directions. But all I saw were a few of the evening news-papers with the latest headlines. I picked them up and slid back into the booth with Akiko and Mae, a little shocked.

"Take a look at this," I said, my voice nearly squeaking. "We're on the front page of the evening newspaper! Flying!"

"But look at that headline," complained Akiko. "What kind of horrible name did they give us?"

"WEE THREE" SAVE THE DAY IN OFFICE BLAZE

Mae seemed to turn away in embarrassment.

"I don't mind that name," she said, unfolding another paper. "It's better than the Super Sprites, which is what they're calling us in this one."

"Or the Caped Kiddies," I offered, pointing at another paper. "That's pretty dreadful."

Akiko's face grew serious, and she ran her finger down the news column on the front page of the *Inquirer*. "Look at this," she began, leaning in closer so she could read the small print. "This story says a kid with a knack for puzzles was kidnapped this morning. Says he was tops in his math class at school. And that he played the violin like a symphony star."

"That's strange," said Mae, sitting up straighter and reading her evening paper. "It says here on page two that another boy was kidnapped just before lunchtime today. His parents report that he was walking home from an appointment at the Carson Building when witnesses saw him pushed into a car."

"The Carson Building?" I said, nearly knocking over my milkshake. "That's where we were today!"

Akiko shook her head and fumbled with her barrette, her bobbed hair swinging. "I don't understand," she said. "Hank Hissler calls for the puzzlers to gather at the Carson Building this morning. Mrs. B catches him giving us a test, so he shuts it down. Then boy puzzlers go missing."

We sat in silence, turning this newest development around and around in our heads. Akiko folded up the papers and shoved them deep into her Hauntima bag.

"Hank Hissler," I said with a shudder. "You don't think he'd vaporize those puzzlers, do you? That he saw how smart the top puzzlers were and felt threatened by them? So he decided to . . ."

Akiko and Mae shook their heads.

"He was excited about them," Mae suggested, trying to connect the dots. "Mr. Hissler wanted to use their smarts."

"But not for Room Twelve business," said Akiko. "I bet he wanted those puzzlers to work for him—doing something dark."

We sat staring at the table in stunned silence for a moment or two.

"It looks like we have at least three mysteries to uncover," I whispered, imagining the newspaper photo of Akiko, Mae, and me soaring through the sky. "First is finding out why these puzzlers have gone missing. Second is figuring out why Hank Hissler betrayed Room Twelve. And th—"

"What's the third?" asked Akiko impatiently, her breathing fast. And loud.

"The third has to do with a *Spion*," I said, glancing around to make sure nobody could hear me. "That's a German word. For *spy*. I think Harry's friends might be up to something!"

Sixteen

THE JANGLY BELLS ABOVE THE DOOR SOUNDED, and they were quickly followed by footsteps racing deep into the diner, all the way to our table.

"It's Emmett! Help!"

I jumped out of the booth just as Emmett's little sister, Audrey, stumbled into me, her words coming in anguished gulps. "He was right out front when a car pulled up. They threw him inside, Josie! They slammed the door and took Emmett away!"

I grabbed Audrey's shoulders and turned her to face me. "Slowly, Audrey. Now explain it to me. Who were they? Did you see their faces? Did you recognize the car?"

"Did Emmett try to escape?" asked Akiko, who suddenly was right beside us with Mae tight on her heels. "Did he struggle?"

Audrey chewed on her lip, looking like she was trying hard not to cry. "It happened so fast," she said, catching her breath. "He was up ahead of me, on the sidewalk. I'd been at my tap-dancing class after school, and I knew he'd be coming here for milkshakes with you, like he always does. At the corner, he stopped to let an old lady cross the street. That's when two men, they pressed in on either side of Emmett. And they pushed him into a car. . . ."

Audrey's voice caught in her throat.

"Did you see what they looked like?" asked Mae gently. "Something that could help identify them? The color of their clothing or maybe a scar on a cheek?"

Audrey shrugged. "They looked like any other goons you can imagine: thick necks holding up meaty heads. Fingers like sausages. But the third guy, he was somebody I'll never forget."

She shivered like it was thirty degrees outside and not a summer evening. "That man, he jumped out and held open his car door. Even though he never took his hat off, I could tell that his head underneath was bald. He wore a gray fedora hat with a black band, and the rim was stiff and sharp—it looked deadly as a blade. His mustache was a straight line, and his glasses were wire circles.

"But those eyes are what scared me," Audrey said, pausing. "They glowed yellow like a snake's."

"Hank Hissler," croaked Akiko.

"It does sound like Mr. Hissler," cautioned Mae, "but how would he even know where to find Emmett?"

A panicky feeling flooded my mind as I replayed the conversation I'd had back in Room Twelve this morning. When Mr. Hissler had asked me about Emmett, I'd bragged that he was my best friend.

I know where and when anybody can find Emmett. We have milkshakes together at five o'clock every afternoon—root beer floats with chocolate ice cream, to be exact. I know because I make them myself.

I may have been salty with Mr. Hissler, but I hadn't given away where he could find Emmett. I was much too smart to do that.

Gerda's cuckoo clock began its noisy routine. We paused, all of us stopping for a moment to listen as the bell chimed five times.

"So, if that was Mr. Hissler who took Emmett," I said, my throat dry as a cotton sock, "how did he know where to find him?"

Little Audrey pointed toward my heart, where GERDA'S DINER was embroidered in green on my crisp white blouse.

"Maybe he read your shirt," she said. "Because the clue is right there for any dumbbell to see."

Seventeen

$\mathcal{W}$HERE ARE WE GOING?" MAE PUFFED AS SHE and Akiko tried to keep up. "And why are we walking so fast? I'm breaking a sweat here, Josie."

My knees trembled as I pushed through the intersection, desperate to spot any sign that Emmett was somehow still around.

"Mae's right, Josie," heaved Akiko, gulping air. "What gives?"

We were walking south on Thirty-Sixth Street, and I was scanning in all directions for the car that took Emmett. How could I have let this happen? It was my fault Emmett had been kidnapped. So it was my job to find him and bring him back safely.

But amid the crush of cars and people, there seemed little hope of spotting him now. By this point, the car that took him was probably speeding through the city. "Emmett!" I shouted desperately into the crowd. "Emmett, where are you?"

I was just turning back toward Gerda's when Mae tugged on my arm.

"Hey, wait a second. Isn't that the Duke?" she whispered, gesturing toward a man getting into a black sedan up ahead of us. "He was at the diner just before Emmett went missing."

"He's the one you said mentioned something about a spy, right?" asked Akiko. "Should we follow him?"

Mae didn't hesitate, not even for a second.

"Of course we should follow him," she declared. "Come on, Josie. Let's go!"

And as the black car drove away, we grabbed one another's hands and raced toward the nearest trolley.

While the worry for Emmett put me in a dark mood, a small glimmer of hope began to burn inside me. Because without even hesitating, Akiko and Mae were ready to jump into action. It was as if leaping onto trolleys and chasing down bad guys were the most natural thing in the world for the three of us to be doing just then.

I gave their hands a quick squeeze, and they squeezed right back.

The Duke's car roared out ahead of the trolley in a puff of gray fumes. Akiko held her nose as I hung off the side and kept an eye on the black sedan's shiny chrome bumper up ahead, the wind whipping my hair.

When another trolley clanged past in the opposite direction, Mae grabbed my waist and yanked me back inside.

"Following that car is great," she huffed. "Getting chopped in half is not!"

Suddenly the traffic backed up, and the trolley pulled up right beside the Duke's car—so close we could reach out and touch it. A bull-nosed driver wearing a chauffeur's cap sat behind the steering wheel and kept his eyes on the road. But in the back seat I could see the Duke. And beside him was a woman who looked to be about the same age as my cousin Kay, early twenties or so. She was blond, and from what I could tell, her hair was pulled back in a modest bun at the nape of her neck. The jacket over her shoulders was green, but that was all I could glimpse of her clothing.

"What if he sees us?" I said, turning my face away. "He might get suspicious."

Akiko plunged her hand into her canvas pouch and rooted around. When she pulled it out, she was holding one of the newspapers from the diner.

"Here, let's hide behind this," she said, unfurling the

paper. Mae and I pressed in close, the newspaper shielding us like a curtain. Slowly the three of us peeked over the top edge.

"I wish their windows were rolled down," whispered Mae. "Can anybody read lips?"

Suddenly the light turned green, and the trolley proceeded up the avenue. Only instead of traveling beside us, now the Duke's black car turned right onto Walnut Street. We were losing him!

"Everybody off!" shouted Mae. "Jump!"

And together we leapt off the moving trolley, landing right in the path of an oncoming trash truck. Its horn blew as the silver grille barreled toward us!

"Run!" shrieked Akiko.

And we did.

Tearing down the block after the black car, we nearly toppled an elderly couple strolling arm in arm. Akiko jumped over a red tricycle pedaled by a toddler, and I barely missed colliding with a baby carriage. Only Mae seemed to be able to navigate the busy street without crashing into anyone. She even managed to pet the head of a Great Dane as she raced past.

"Can't we just transform into superheroes again?" asked Akiko between puffs of air. "Flying would be easier than running!"

"We don't have time to transform," I answered. "Plus, I'm not sure how we did it in the first place!" Not to mention whether we even should. What would it do to Mam if I were to get vaporized? *Stay safe. No trouble.*

"He's turning left at that next corner," Mae called over her shoulder. "Cut through the park!"

We veered left into a leafy park and careened down the gravelly path, Mae at the front, me barely holding steady on her heels, and poor Akiko heaving and wheezing somewhere behind us.

When we finally reached the sidewalk at the other end of the gardens, we collapsed onto a wooden bench just steps away from the shiny black sedan and the bull-nosed driver. He had parked along the street across from a low-slung redbrick building.

"Does anybody even know where we are?" asked Mae, who seemed to be too polite to break a sweat.

"Walnut Street," I said, tilting my head to look up at the post that was just a few feet away on the corner. The sign on top was easy to read. "And Thirty-Third Street."

Huffing and heaving and trying to catch our breath, the three of us watched as the blond lady climbed out of the car and the Duke rolled down his window to speak with her.

"What's he saying?" Akiko asked, still panting open-mouthed. "Can you hear him?"

"Not with you breathing so loud in my ear," answered Mae. "But look, I think that's a clue."

The Duke, who had never seemed too bright to me, was

counting on his fingers—*one, two, three, four, five, six.* Then he pointed over at the redbrick building. The blond woman nodded, adjusted the collar of her green jacket, then headed for the building. Once she stepped inside, the Duke's car rolled away, slinking like a shark down the street.

"Six," I whispered. "You're right, Mae. The Duke is interested in six of something inside that building."

"There's a sign near the door," Akiko said, pointing. "Let's go see what this place is. Maybe we can start piecing clues together."

Crossing the street and heading toward the big wooden doors, we tried not to draw attention to ourselves. When the building's sign came into view, all three of us stopped and stared:

MOORE SCHOOL OF ELECTRICAL ENGINEERING

UNIVERSITY OF PENNSYLVANIA

We were turning away to race back toward the bench again when a slim figure up ahead caught my eye. It was a woman wearing a red beret and carrying a red pocketbook, and she was approaching the Moore School on the sidewalk just steps from us. A broken tree branch was blocking her path, but she leapt over it, graceful as a doe.

"Wait a minute! I'd know that hat and that jump anywhere! She looks like . . ."

I slipped behind a tree, and Akiko and Mae followed. Peeking our three heads around the grainy bark, we studied her. She'd stopped near the front step and was chatting with a few friends. Then one of them pulled open the heavy wooden door and they all stepped inside, comfortable rather than cautious, like they were familiar with the place.

"That's Kay," I whispered. "That's my cousin!"

My hands trembled as I clutched Mae's arm on one side, Akiko's on the other.

"Does Kay know the Duke?" asked Mae urgently.

"Does she know that blond lady?" added Akiko. "The Duke's spy?"

My mind was a spinning record player. Was Kay in danger too, like Emmett? I had to keep her safe, but what was she doing here? What if she crossed paths with the Duke or one of his thick-necked bullies? Or that horrible Mr. Hissler?

Kay was supposed to be working at the market this time of day. She was supposed to be running the cash register and giving people change for a quarter. She wasn't supposed to be hanging around a place like this, not when the Duke was up to something here.

"The Moore School? Engineering?" I whispered, barely keeping up. "I have no idea what's going on. But I can say this confirms my suspicion: I don't think Cousin Kay is ringing up groceries!"

Eighteen

WE STARED AT THE ENGINEERING SCHOOL. Now that we knew what Mr. Hissler had done to the Stretcher, Emmett almost certainly was in grave danger. And now what about Kay?

Thoughts of Emmett ricocheted through my mind like a bouncy ball. Should we scour the city and call his name? Should we race back to the Carson Building in search of Mr. Hissler for answers? Should we contact Mrs. B and Astra for help?

Images from my comic books played through my mind—scenes where the evildoers were vanquished. That might happen with Hauntima, Hopscotch, and Nova the Sunchaser. But with Cousin Kay?

"You two wait over there," I said, pointing back across the street at our bench. "I'll go poke around inside and talk to Kay, and then I'll come right back. It won't take very long."

I tiptoed out from behind the cottonwood and headed for the engineering school's doors. But I wasn't moving alone. I could feel Akiko and Mae right with me. I didn't protest, though, since I was just as nosy as they were. I would have done exactly the same thing. And having them beside me made my steps a little sturdier.

The first floor was silent as we edged around the empty foyer. Suddenly a door opened at the end of a long hallway, and a man in a dark suit stepped out. The last thing I wanted was to explain what we were doing sneaking around an engineering school, so I bolted up the nearest staircase. Mae and Akiko took the stairs two at a time beside me.

On the second floor, the sounds of a busy office drifted out to us from behind the closed doors. Wasn't it time to go home for the day? I caught women's voices chatting here and there, but mostly what we heard was a constant clicking noise, like hundreds of forks tapping on hundreds of plates.

Suddenly one of the doors swung open, and the clicking grew louder as a woman swept into the hallway and nearly crashed right into us.

"Children? Good golly, what are y'all doing here?" she asked, not unfriendly but not particularly welcoming either. "This isn't exactly a place I'd expect to see kids."

She seemed maybe twenty years old or so, with fire-engine-red hair that was probably wild like mine but instead appeared tamed, pinned back in a neat style. A pencil stuck out from behind her left ear, and I noticed one of her hands was smudged with ink.

"Josie is looking for her cousin," announced Akiko, prodding me in the ribs with her bony elbow. "Kay is her name. Know her?"

Mae looked as if she wanted to pop a cork in Akiko's mouth and bottle up all her words. She stepped forward, shouldering Akiko out of the way ever so slightly, and gave the Southern-sounding lady a polite nod.

"What my friend meant to say, ma'am," she began in a voice that was wrapped in pretty paper and tied up with a neat bow, "is Josie here missed her chance to wish Kay a happy birthday. And to make up for it, she wanted to stop by and let her know what a wonderful cousin she's been to Josie and her baby brothers."

For as proper as she looked, Mae was surprisingly good at being sneaky.

"Well, sakes alive! Kay McNulty's cousin? And a birthday?" the lady said, pushing past us with a quick step and proceeding down another hallway. "Follow me, y'all, and I'll settle you into one of the offices. My name is Jean Jennings, and I happen to work with Kay. We're in the basement now, doing what we can for a new project. But I can't let you children down there. I'll bring Kay upstairs to you."

Jean opened a door and waved us in. Her hands gesturing toward a desk at the back of the room, she told us to make ourselves at home. Then she headed for the door again, promising to track down Kay.

This room was filled with that same clicking sound, only louder now that we were so close. I stared all around to figure out what it was. Rows and rows of women were seated at desks, their hands and fingers flying over calculating machines. The clicking must have been coming from all the buttons being punched.

"What are they doing?" whispered Akiko, clearly baffled. "It looks like they're typing."

I paused, watching the women closely. Is this what Kay was up to? Ringing up numbers, only not at our neighborhood grocery store? I couldn't make sense of it all.

On chalkboards around the room were written complicated math equations and charts. And at every wooden desk were small adding machines with loads of buttons. So many women tapping on so many buttons created the odd-sounding symphony we'd heard all the way downstairs.

"Calculators!" I whispered, a little too noisily. "All these women must be busy computing math problems."

As I gazed around the room, my eyes were suddenly drawn to something other than the calculating machines. They were fixed on a blond head and a green jacket seated two rows over. The Duke's friend!

Could she really be the spy he was talking about? What about his counting up to six? Six spies? There were so many numbers written on chalkboards around this room. What was the significance of the number six?

Moments later the door opened, and my cousin marched in, with Jean following close behind her.

"Josie," Kay said, not really scolding but not exactly happy to see me. "What are you doing here? You know my birthday is February twelfth, not today."

"I—I forgot," I stammered. Now that we were inside the Moore School, I had no idea what we should do. "D-d-do you want to go for cake anyway?"

Kay looked at me like I was crazy.

Thoughts began playing bumper cars in my mind. I didn't know where to even start. What could I say to Kay? That we thought a spy had sneaked into her office? That we were looking for my best friend, Emmett, who seemed to have been kidnapped? That we wanted to know what exactly she was doing in this office to begin with, since it wasn't Caruso's Market and there were no apples or cucumbers or milk pints to be seen anywhere? Not to mention the little detail that I had superpowers and so did my two new friends?

I rattled my head back and forth, hoping to dislodge some sort of decent-sounding idea. "We just wanted to s-say hello," I stammered, staring up into her steady eyes. "We were in the neighborhood—"

Akiko interrupted, too impatient to wait her turn.

"What is this place?" she said, looking all around the room. "I mean, what are all these women doing with the adding machines?"

Kay stared at me for a beat or two, silence hanging heavy in the air. She had no idea how I had found her, but she was too polite to press me on it in front of everyone. I was relieved when she finally spoke.

"I guess it won't hurt for you to know," Kay began, her eyes sweeping the room from one side to the other. "I didn't want you and your brothers trumpeting it to the neighborhood, so I never told you when I stopped working at the market. But I work here now.

"The women you see around us, we're mathematicians—some of us with degrees from colleges and others who came on board just because they love math and are good at it." I thought I noticed a glimmer of pride as she spoke. "We use these machines to calculate complicated math problems.

"We're computers."

Then Jean stepped closer, adding to Kay's explanation with her Southern twang. "The problems y'all see these ladies solving right here," she said, pointing at a row of women computers near us, "are what soldiers will use in the field to fire their guns and drop their bombs on the enemy."

I eyed the pens and pencils on the desks nearby. I recognized the long slide rules and sharp-tipped mathematics compasses used for working out complicated equations. I picked up a sheet of paper and a pencil from an empty desk and held it up for Mae and Akiko to read too. "I don't understand. You're doing math—to help fight the Nazis?" I asked, keeping half an eye on Kay to make sure she didn't show signs of wanting to strangle me.

While I knew Kay loved me, I also knew I could drive her crazy now and then with all my nosiness, eavesdropping, and general butting-into-her-business.

"A shell can get knocked off course by wind, cloudy weather—lots of things," Kay explained patiently. "The computers—these women you see right here—change up the math equations and figure out how the soldiers should set their weapons if it's rainy or stormy.

"To hand-compute just one of these trajectories," she said, reaching over and touching one of the calculators on a desk, "takes us about thirty or forty hours of putting pencil to paper and tapping numbers into a calculator. Then we put all our calculations into booklets and ship them off to the front lines for the soldiers."

My jaw dropped nearly to the floor. To think of my

sharp-as-a-sewing-needle cousin ringing up milk sales at a market seemed ridiculous now. She was so much more than that. She was a computer—a *human* computer!

Kay loved math, puzzles, and patterns the same way I did. Sometimes when she was relaxing after a shift, we would sit at the kitchen table together, and she'd serve me a cup of tea, a shortbread cookie, and a problem to solve. At this point, she had me doing algebra already. Kay said I could be a mathematician like her one day if I wanted to.

When this war is over . . . , she'd always say.

There were so many things we'd do when this war was over.

Mae was staring at one of the computers in particular, though her good manners meant she wouldn't point. "What about her?" she asked gently, tugging on my arm. And to my surprise, she wasn't looking over at the blonde in green whom we'd seen with the Duke. Mae was looking at someone else entirely.

"She looks just like my mother," Mae said. "Is she a computer like all the others?"

Kay and Jean nodded, telling us that this group had been picked from colleges all over the country. Because most of the men were overseas fighting, women math majors were asked to do their part.

I craned my neck to get a look at who had caught Mae's attention, and Akiko stepped into the aisle for a better peek too. From what I could see, it was a youngish black woman seated at the far side of the room along the windows. Her hair was stylish, and she wore a neat rose-colored blouse tucked into a dark skirt. When she turned to chat with the woman working beside her, I noticed her eyes were soft and even a little shy.

"That's Alyce Hall," said Kay.

"Her sister Alma is a mathematician too," Jean pointed out. "Two mathematicians in one family? Can you imagine?"

I looked right at Kay and held my breath. Because I imagined it every day.

Nineteen

RIGHT-E-O. LET'S GET BACK TO THE POINT, Josie," Kay said, her hands on her hips now and her patience running thin. "What are you doing here—"

"I haven't even introduced you to my puzzler friends," I said quickly, hoping to dodge that question. How could I explain how we found her this evening? If we involved Kay, surely we'd be putting her and the other computers in danger. The Duke was already nosing around. What if he did something to Kay? The thought made me shudder. "Kay," I said, my voice tight, "meet Akiko and Mae."

"So you made the cut?" Kay asked, the irritation on her

face finally softening now. "All three of you? You passed the puzzle tests?"

I hated to disappoint Kay, and I guess my expression said enough. I stared down at the floor. Akiko and Mae went silent.

"Oh, I'm sorry, Josie," she said, patting my arm. "That's a shame, when you studied so hard for it. I bet you girls did too."

"It's okay," said Mae, a little too brightly. "We met each other. And we've had plenty of other adventures—er, I mean, things—to keep us busy today."

"No, it's not really okay," corrected Akiko, folding her arms across her chest with a cranky huff. "Mae likes to wrap everything in rainbows. The instructor only looked at the boys' exams this morning. So we didn't make the cut, and that really stinks."

"Right, but we've gotten to know each other," said Mae, raising her eyebrows at Akiko and trying to say something without *really* saying something. "And everything else made the time *fly*. . . ."

"Right!" exclaimed Akiko, as if she'd forgotten all about our superpowers. "Exactly! Who cares about those tests?"

I was standing between Akiko and Mae, but I certainly didn't want to get caught between them as they squabbled or babbled or whatever it was they were doing. My eyes shot over to the blonde in the green coat again. I felt certain she was working for the Duke and spying on the computers. But I didn't know how to prove my suspicions were real and not the wild imaginings of a comic book fan.

Kay could be in danger! And Jean and the other women too!

I let out a frustrated sigh. We needed to get Kay and the others away from this place. For just a few days or so. Then we could focus on finding Emmett, catching Mr. Hissler, and stopping whatever scheming the Duke was up to.

"Well, thanks for the visit, Josie," said Kay, "but it's time you three—"

"Allow me to explain a bit," Mae began in her polished, charm-school way. "Josie here worries so much about how hard you work. She just, well . . . She was thinking it might do you some good to take a day off."

"Not a day off," corrected Akiko firmly. "When you put it that way, it sounds like a vacation. We're talking about possible danger, Mae." Akiko might have thought she was whispering, but her voice was loud enough for all of us to hear. "It could come from anywhere! Even that evil mastermind Hank Hissler!"

Kay suddenly wrapped her arms around my shoulders and ushered me toward the door, with Jean shepherding Mae and Akiko behind us. Hushing our protests and offering apologies to the other women at their desks as we stumbled past, they quickly moved us out into the hallway, then shut the door firmly behind them.

"This sounds a little like a comic book story, don't you think? Complete with danger and an evil villain." Jean chuckled. "Didn't you tell me she was obsessed with that caped hero Zenobia? And her sister—what's her name?"

"The Palomino," answered the three of us.

"Look, Josie," Kay said in a fierce whisper, "we don't have time for silly games. You girls talk about danger. Well, of course there is danger—a war is on! All of us have to pitch in as best we can."

"And for your cousin Kay and me," added Jean, her words coming in a slow drawl, "the way we can fight this war is with our brains. You children are young, and you might not understand the seriousness of what's at stake. But for Kay and me and the others, what we're doing here is important work."

"When it comes to beating our enemies," Kay said, gesturing toward the women computers behind the door, "math is a powerful weapon!"

The sound of shoes tapping up the hallway toward us grabbed our attention, and we fell to silence. A tall, thin man was walking our way. As he passed, he gave Kay and Jean a quick nod and said something about a meeting on their new project in the basement. It was happening in a few minutes, he said, turning his wrist to glance at his watch. And as he did, I caught a glimpse of the folder in his arms. It read, CONFIDENTIAL: PROJECT PX.

"Listen, Josie, I know you have a pretty good imagination," Kay began. "And sometimes your stories . . . Well, I think of them like taffy: The truth gets stretched and pulled."

More women rounded the corner, and my cousin thankfully went silent about my imagination. The group greeted Jean and Kay, eyebrows raised at the sight of us. Two of them were holding the same folder I'd seen before, PROJECT PX emblazoned across the front. Kay looked embarrassed and began moving us toward the staircase that led to the front door, eager to clear us out.

"My little cousin and her friends," she said by way of introduction, awkwardly turning to speak to them. "Girls, these are my colleagues—Marlyn, Ruth, Betty, and Fran."

One, two, three, four, I counted. And with Kay and Jean, *five, six.*

Unlike the Duke, I could do it in my head instead of on my fingers.

Six computers on a special, secret project.

A moment later, a door shut and another woman joined them from the calculating room. It was the blonde in the green jacket—the Duke's friend.

"And this is Ursula," Kay said, with a friendly nod in the blonde's direction. "She's new but very good."

The three of us stared wide-eyed at Ursula for a beat or two. Then we began a bit of curtsying and nodding and hand-shaking with the whole group, thrilled at the chance to meet these computers in person. Not to mention being so close to a possible spy.

"Listen, Josie." Kay started again, turning away from her colleagues and leaning in close to my ear. "You aren't supposed to know anything about what's going on here, about the computers or the project Jean and I and these others are working on. Nothing. What we're doing here is important. And confidential. I appreciate your concern, but I cannot have children popping around playing games down the hallways."

"But if you're playing softball, I'm in." Jean, who was leaning close to Kay and me now too, laughed. "I'm a great pitcher."

Kay gave me a firm look and nodded toward the front door.

"Goodbye, Josie," she said, waving over her shoulder as she headed off toward the other women. "I have no idea how you found me today. But please don't worry. Very few people know about this place. We're safe."

"It was a pleasure to meet y'all," added Jean with a polite bow, and I noticed now that she had one of the evening newspapers tucked under her arm. I could read the "Wee Three" headline blaring above the photo that featured the three of us in our capes, masks, and boots in the Carson Building's courtyard.

"Now, if you want an exciting story," Jean said, unfolding her newspaper and tapping the headline, "keep a lookout for these superheroes who showed up in town. I sure wish I could work with them for an hour or two. I'd calculate their flight trajectories!"

And with that Jean turned and joined my cousin and the others. I stared after them, watching their shapes disappear down the staircase.

Six women mathematicians. Six human computers. My instincts told me not to count the Duke's friend Ursula among them.

"What do you think they're up to?" I whispered to Mae and Akiko as the echo of the computers' footsteps faded. "Their folders said 'Project PX.' I wonder why it's marked 'confidential.'"

"We'd better go," Mae said softly as she tried to move us toward the door. "Come on, Josie, let's get out of here."

"Mae is right," agreed Akiko. "You don't want to get your cousin mad at us."

"Sure," I whispered, "we can go. But only after I take a peek at where they're heading. The Secret Six. Don't you want to know more? Don't you want to keep an eye on the blond lady? That Ursula?"

With silent footsteps, I tiptoed down the staircase. Leaning over the railing, I listened to the murmur of the voices chatting down below. I heard a door shut, then silence.

"I'll be right back," I called in a hushed shout over my shoulder.

"You don't have to be so loud," said Akiko, her face suddenly inches from mine. "We're right here."

"Did you honestly think we'd let you do this alone?" said Mae beside her.

I couldn't stop the grin that took over my cheeks. Together we slinked down the staircase and along the basement hallway. The closed wooden doors all looked the same. Finally, the last one showed promise.

"That has to be the one," I whispered, trying not to shout. "Look!"

A big sign hammered onto the door warned us away:

HIGH VOLTAGE: KEEP OUT!

"We can't exactly barge in there and sit down at their secret meeting," Akiko said tightly. "We'll just have to come back, maybe when nobody is around."

"But someone is probably always around if this project is so top secret," whispered Mae, looking nervously up and down the hallway.

"You're right. We can't just barge in," I said, finally surrendering. "Let's get out of this place. But promise me we'll come right back here and check this out tomorrow. Even if the Duke and Ursula aren't up to bad things, I still want to find out what makes this project so secret."

We quietly tiptoed back up the staircase, then we dashed out the front door.

The sun had set, but the sky still glowed in the west. We crossed the street and began our walk home. "We have so many things to figure out," Mae said. "Project PX, the Duke, Ursula—"

"Mr. Hissler, Mrs. B, Astra," added Akiko, "and of course, finding your friend Emmett."

We passed a newspaper stand on the corner selling the day's papers. The headlines caught my eye.

"WEE THREE" CAPED KIDS SAVE

DOZENS IN OFFICE FIRE

"Let's head to my apartment for the night," I said, feeling a little woozy as I peered up at the first stars twinkling overhead. "I have to watch my little brothers while Mam and Kay work late shifts. Maybe you both can spend the night, and we can talk through everything that's happened today. Because aside from all you named, there's something else we have to figure out."

"What's that?" they both asked.

"Us."

Twenty

$\mathcal{W}$E WERE ALMOST TO MY APARTMENT WHEN
Mae and Akiko ducked into the phone booth at Mr. Hunter's
barbershop to call their families. Mae's grandmother was
just closing up at the library where she worked, and after
much begging and sweet-talking and apologizing for missing
supper—as well as telling Granny she had something early
tomorrow morning having to do with puzzler work—Mae
finally convinced Granny Crumpler to allow a sleepover at
my apartment. Akiko's aunt and uncle were so busy closing
up their store and rounding up all of Akiko's cousins that
they said yes right away.

By the time we climbed to the third floor and stepped

into my apartment, we were exhausted. The radio blared from its corner stand in the dining room, and a war correspondent was reporting on an Allied battle against the Nazis. *"By land and by air, American and Allied forces are overpowering the Nazi army at every turn!"* the reporter shouted. *"Even in heavy winds and rains, bombs are striking with pinpoint accuracy."*

Pinpoint accuracy.

I thought of Kay and the other women computers.

"I'm home!" I hollered.

My little brothers came running full speed down the hallway toward us, their arms outstretched like they were imaginary bombers on their own flying missions against the enemy.

Our apartment was small, so there wasn't really a need for yelling. But with the constant noise and commotion that came with my family, shouting was sometimes the only way to get anybody's attention.

"I hear you," came Mam's exasperated reply. "How was the diner today?"

She greeted me in the hallway, familiar teacup in her hands and singsongy lilt in her voice. Even though we emigrated from Ireland, nobody could detect an Irish accent in my voice—except Akiko, I guess. But with Mam, just a simple *yes* or *no* revealed rolling green fields and rainy coastlines. "Goodness, what a surprise! You've brought friends home. How do you do, girls?"

Mam stuck her palm out and gave Akiko's hand a firm shake. Then she did the same with Mae, who added a little curtsy too. I was beginning to suspect Mae's granny wasn't a librarian but rather headmistress of a charm school. Mam was clearly impressed.

"You're a bit late tonight, Josephine," she said, cupping one warm hand to my cheek while she balanced her teacup in the other. "I was worried. But I can see you're safe and sound."

Mam's eyes looked tired and her face thin.

"Kay won't be home until midnight, and I'll be soon after. Now, I'm late for work already, so mind the boys." And then, lowering her voice so my brothers couldn't hear, she added, "That awful landlord Mr. Hunter stopped by today to complain about the noise. We can't have him upset, so keep it quiet up here tonight. And please, Josie, stay safe. No trouble."

With the war on, my mom had taken a second job—working the late shift at the naval shipyard, helping build battleships and things. It sounded boring to me, but she got along well with the other women. And the pay was good, though not as good as her day job at the veterinary clinic.

"The kettle's on for tea," she called from the kitchen. I knew she was searching for her pocketbook. "And there's the stew you made yesterday. You can serve it to your friends."

"Only if she wants to kill them!" shouted Vinnie. Then

he announced, to nobody in particular, the gory details of food poisoning. "Vomiting, stomach pain, diarrhea, fever. And that's just from bad meat. Now, potatoes, they can be just as deadly. . . ."

"Jothie's food is poithon!" joined Baby Lou, dropping to the floor and pretending to gag. Since he'd lost his two front teeth, Lou had lost his *S*, too. "We won't touch the th-tuff!"

Nobody appreciated my cooking around here. But to be perfectly honest, neither did I. The meals I made were pretty wretched. Thank goodness for Gerda's pies and milk-shakes.

"My friends need to sleep here tonight," I told Mam, trying not to lie but definitely not giving away anything about Room Twelve. "We're . . . working on a complicated project. It has to do with . . . puzzle solving. We might have to run through some problems tomorrow morning. . . ."

Since Mae was visiting from Chicago and Akiko had just moved here from San Francisco, they were already out of school for summer. But my school still had another agonizing day before summer vacation started. I had no intention of going—not with Emmett missing and all the other questions swirling in the air. But if I got caught, my mother would never let me leave the house again.

"Set your alarm clock so you don't oversleep," Mam called from the other side of the bathroom door. "But it's straight to school afterward. You can't be missing lessons, even on the last day. There's nothing you could possibly do tomorrow that's more important than school."

I heard Akiko gulp, her noisy breathing suddenly silent. Mae let out a little gasp. If my mom only knew.

She hustled out of the bathroom again, slid into her shoes at the same time she knotted a scarf over her hair, then kissed me on the forehead. Mam always seemed to be in motion. "Mercy me! I forgot to pack a late supper," she sang, rushing off to the kitchen. "Good luck to you on the puzzling, Josie. You're as brilliant as Kay."

Being smart was everything to my mother—not just making good grades, but really knowing things. When my family left Ireland, none of us children spoke a word of English. We'd been born in an Irish-speaking region in the west. But once we had landed here in the United States, Mam was determined that all us kids would go to school, learn English and everything we could, and make successes of ourselves.

"It's the American way," she liked to tell us with a wink. "And when you're all big shots, you'll buy me boxes of chocolates for Christmas each year. That's the American way too—treating your mother like a queen!"

But life is full of curlicues.

My mom could see us making something of ourselves in school. But what she couldn't foresee was the war taking my father away, leaving her to raise Vinnie, Lou, and me on her own.

Or me having to take a job to help her do it.

Mam felt bad about that, but I didn't mind so much. And really, what choice did we have when stomachs were in need of feeding, little brothers were outgrowing their shoes and pants and shirts, and rents to that awful Mr. Hunter— terrible Toby's dad—were always coming due? Thank goodness my cousin Kay was around to help us.

"How many of you are there?" asked Mae, careful not to trip over my brothers, who had decided it was a good time to start wrestling on the floor before us.

"We're as loud as twenty. But aside from my mom, there're just two boys and two girls," I said, stepping over to separate my brothers. "You met my cousin Kay and, of course, me. Then there's this one here," I continued, grabbing Vinnie by the arm and pulling him to his feet, "with the fresh black eye he must have gotten today after school, playing too rough at basketball—he's Vincent."

"Not at basketball! I got it from Lou about an hour ago," hollered Vinnie, diving onto the living room sofa and hiding beneath my favorite green blanket. Then, peeking out, he asked Mae and Akiko, "Do you want to know the best way to treat a black eye? You put a metal spoon in the icebox so it's nice and cold, then press the back of the spoon to the injured part around your eye. Cold compression is what you're after."

Mae was clearly impressed—having Vinnie around was

like having your very own walking, talking bookshelf. He was filled with facts. I bet Mae's granny would love him.

"And this little angel is Louis," I said, giving his pudgy cheeks a pinch.

"He looks just like you," said Mae, running her finger along her nose and cheekbones. "Same face, same hair. You both resemble your mom."

"And Vinnie lookth like our dad," chirped Baby Lou just before diving onto the couch beside his big brother.

"Is this him?" asked Akiko, who had been slowly making her way around the room, from the photographs on the bookshelves to those on the fireplace mantel and then to the radio, staring into the faces. She glanced over at Vinnie and smiled, then turned back to the picture hanging on the wall. "In his uniform like that, he reminds me of my brother, Tommy."

"Our daddy fought at Pearl Harbor," said Baby Lou, who had decided to sit upside down on the sofa now.

"He's a hero," added Vinnie in his serious way, perched on the sofa's arm next to Lou. "The Japanese sunk eighteen ships that day, including five battleships. Our dad saved one of them. He got a medal for it."

Akiko looked across the room at me, her eyes sorrowful.

"It was a terrible day," she whispered. "I'm so sorry he was there."

I shrugged. I didn't want to go into it all, not with my

little brothers around. "He's fought lots of battles in the Pacific," I said, reaching out to Vinnie's mop of dark hair and tousling it. "Our dad is like Captain Flexor. Right, boys?"

My brothers cheered and tumbled off the sofa for another wrestling match as my mom stood in the living room doorway, draping a light sweater over her shoulders. Her expression was pained as we held each other's gaze for a moment or two.

She looked so weary.

"I'll be home from the shipyard before you wake, love," she said. I stepped over to give her one last hug. "Just put them to bed soon and tuck them in. And I cooked a supper too, since the boys complained so much about your . . ." Then she caught herself. My lamb stew was famously bad. "Well, what I mean is, you have options for supper tonight. A liver loaf is warming in the oven, and buttered spinach is on the stove top. The boys have eaten already. At least I think they have."

She planted another kiss on my forehead. "Stay safe. No trouble," she whispered—to me if not to heaven.

I'd try.

But I couldn't make any guarantees.

Twenty-One

LIVER LOAF? AND SPINACH?

I glanced over my shoulder toward the sofa table and spotted a plate of Lorna Doone shortbread cookies. Vinnie and Baby Lou were setting up a game of Parcheesi now, cookie crumbs dotting their faces as they called goodbye to Mam. It was clear to me what my little brothers were really eating for dinner, and it wasn't liver loaf. Or spinach.

The radio was playing, and both my brothers bopped their heads to the music. I could hear Baby Lou singing along with Bing Crosby about swinging on a star and moonbeams in a jar.

"Stars are big, exploding balls of gas," I heard Vinnie

explain. "So we couldn't really swing on them. Plus, they're about ten thousand degrees, so they'd be really hot to touch."

Baby Lou agreed, his mouth full of cookies. "Ex-thactly," he said. Or something close to that.

I gestured silently toward the kitchen, and Mae, Akiko, and I backed away from the boys as if they were sleeping giants. If Vinnie and Baby Lou kept themselves busy, then the three of us could talk without being interrupted every five minutes.

I pulled my lamb stew from the icebox and scooped out heaping helpings. Pouring tea into cups, I listened as Akiko and Mae began testing each other's puzzling abilities.

"That cipher is so easy, Akiko," Mae scoffed, her pencil flying across Akiko's paper. "All you did was drop the vowels. I was solving these kinds of things in second grade!"

Akiko folded up her notebook and tucked it back into her Hauntima bag. She adjusted her barrette with a little huff of irritation.

"We have so many things to figure out," I began, setting the bowls onto the table. "Like poor Emmett! I can't stop worrying about him. Do you think Mr. Hissler wants to use him and the other boys for something bad?"

Akiko sniffed at the stew, her face crinkling up like a prune. But ever-polite Mae nibbled on a bite and gave me a half-hearted smile. "Nice," she said, though she looked pained.

I offered to heat it up.

"No, no," they both said, waving their hands. "That won't be necessary."

Scenes from our day tumbled through my mind. "So who made the Stretcher go missing?" I wondered. "Mr. Hissler probably did it. But he seemed to be running away when the Stretcher was vaporized. Was someone else behind it?"

"And why was Hauntima just a ghost of herself?" said Akiko, scowling into her stew. "And what about the other superheroes? Where have they gone?"

We were quiet for a bit, lost in our thoughts.

"I understand why you're so worried about Emmett, Josie," said Mae, politely pushing her spoon around in her bowl, probably to give me the impression she was eating. "Mr. Hissler made my hair stand on end. And then there's the Duke and his spying on the computers."

She began pacing the kitchen, tugging on her dinner napkin.

"So much has happened today. It makes me feel like I've known you both my whole life," she said, her words coming fast. "But I'm confused, and my head is pounding.

"I went to the Carson Building to see about the position they'd advertised, calling for puzzle solvers. I love Granny Crumpler with all my heart, but I cannot sit through another summer with her and all her books. Whether it's at home in Chicago or here, where she's helping set up the new library." Finally, Mae seemed to drop her formal manner and show us her real feelings.

"I want to do something! I *need* to do something," she continued, her voice rising. "My daddy's over there, living in danger every day. I'd hoped to help the war effort as a puzzler and do my part to fight back against the evil that's gripping this world. But then this happened," she exclaimed, throwing her hands in the direction of Akiko and me. "You. Me. Us!

"And all I can say is that today felt pretty amazing! Is it really possible that we could have powers like Hauntima? Be as strong as the Palomino? Be as bold as Hopscotch and Nova the Sunchaser?" She took a gulp of tea. "Maybe—and this is dreaming—but maybe someday we could even be as inspiring as Zenobia."

My heart raced like I was on my bike and pedaling at full speed. I didn't feel smart enough or brave enough to wear a cape. And there was no way I could ever be considered in the same breath as Zenobia or the others.

"There's some sort of mistake," I whispered into my teacup. "Emmett's kidnapping is my fault. I gave away too much about him. And that's not something a real superhero would do. So I don't think I'm the right person for this. I think somebody else is supposed to be with you two."

Akiko scoffed and pushed back from the table.

"You don't think you're the right person?" she said, her

voice tight. "Look at me! I can hardly breathe half the time because of my asthma and allergies. And I could barely perform the special power I'm supposed to have. If anybody is the mistake, it's me!"

Mae picked up the teakettle and brought it to the table. She refilled Akiko's cup, then mine. Finally, she spoke. And her voice was serious.

"Neither one of you is a mistake. And I'm not either. We three were chosen for a reason—maybe we'll never know why, but there must have been a reason. And I think Mrs. B has something to do with it."

Mae was all business now. Her words came slowly, barely above a whisper, as she took her seat at the table again.

"The cape, mask, and boots we found lying on the floor," she began. "What if they didn't have power from the Stretcher alone? What if the power lingering in the air and on those pieces came from—"

"Jothie?" Suddenly another voice was in the kitchen with us. It was Baby Lou. And he was dragging my green blanket behind him. "Vinnie'th falling asleep, but I need a story. Will you come tell us one?"

"Tell the story about Daddy on the battleship," Vinnie said, his eyes barely open as he appeared behind Lou, leaning his sleepy head against the doorframe.

I got to my feet and turned Vinnie and Lou around. As

much as I wanted to stay up late talking with Akiko and Mae, my brothers needed me tonight. And tucking them under a blanket and telling them a bedtime story was the best way I knew how to protect them from all the bad stuff in the world.

Twenty-Two

MAE, AKIKO, AND I WOKE EARLY THE NEXT morning and quietly slipped out the door, heading right down the block to Gerda's for breakfast. Before we left, I wrote Mam a quick note and adjusted the green blanket over the sleeping forms of Vinnie and Baby Lou. She'd have to walk them to school this morning.

"We've got to watch for the Duke today," Akiko said in her sandpaper voice as we crossed the street. "Does he usually eat breakfast at Gerda's?"

I nodded, looking up and down the block for any sign of him or his black sedan. I even looked for Emmett, though I wasn't too hopeful we'd run into him on Captain

Flexor Street. I'd have to ask Harry what he knew about the Duke. Harry was a good guy. Surely he was suspicious of the Duke too.

"And we've got to beware of Mr. Hissler," Mae whispered, leaning in and making sure nobody could overhear her. "He might want to snatch one of us."

"Doubtful," Akiko said. "He didn't think we were good enough puzzlers."

"We're plenty good," Mae said. "But maybe it's better that he never looked closely at our exams after all. I'd sure hate to be in his clutches."

The bell over the diner door jangled as we walked into the restaurant. Gerda smiled warmly and pointed toward a back booth. "Harry will be glad to see you," she said, picking up a coffeepot and following us to our usual booth. "He's a little *verschroben*," she whispered. Then, just to Akiko and Mae, she explained. "How would you say it in English? *Cranky?*"

We slid into the booth and looked around. Gerda said she'd bring us the usual—plus some scrambled eggs. There were morning newspapers on the table from diners who had been sitting here before us, and Gerda stacked them to throw away. But we told her not to worry—the more news we could read, the better.

The diner was busy with the breakfast crowd, and I promised Gerda I would try to come in later today and help out. I could tell she could use the extra hands. And I could always use the extra money.

"Get a load of this headline," said Akiko as she pointed to an article in one of the morning papers, her laugh like a deflating tire. "The reporter calls us the Power Pixies. Can you believe it? What a ridiculous name!"

We fell quiet as we looked through the stack. There were four different papers, and we were on the front pages of all of them.

"This paper calls us the Daughters of Hauntima!" said Mae, nearly shrieking in her excitement. "I like that name!"

It had been Mae's idea to stop by Gerda's Diner for breakfast before heading for the Carson Building in search of Mrs. B. I could tell that she and Akiko were starving. Even though we had a whole pot of the lamb stew still waiting back at my apartment, not to mention my mom's liver and spinach, neither Akiko nor Mae had eaten last night.

"This one calls us the Tremendous Tykes," I said, pinching my nose. "I'd say that one stinks. What else do you see?"

Gerda returned balancing plates and drinks. We slurped our milkshakes as we scanned the newspapers for more stories about yesterday's fire and the caped kids who saved the day. I loved seeing a photo of me carrying one of the heavy men over my shoulder and another of Mae rescuing the cat.

"What's the deal with running pictures of you two,

when it's clear we're a trio?" demanded Akiko, practically shouting. I kicked her under the table and signaled for her to lower her voice. She was going to get our secret exposed before we even had a decent name! And who knew whether we could make yesterday's superpowers return?

It seemed to be annoying Akiko that she didn't have as many powers as Mae and me. "Josie has superstrength and telekinesis," she complained, "and Mae's got mental telepathy and the power to create storms."

"Atmokinesis," said Mae. "That's its technical name."

Akiko gave her the stink eye. She clearly knew the technical name too.

"Well, where's my second power?" Akiko demanded in a huffy whisper. Then she paused for three quick sneezes. "All I got was shape-shifting. It's not fair!"

"Shape-shifting is one of the best superpowers possible," I whispered, trying to console her. Then I held up a different newspaper. "And look! Here's a photograph that features all three of us. Not bad, right?"

The picture showed Akiko, Mae, and me in flight, soaring above the office building's rooftop. Akiko seemed satisfied and dropped the subject.

"Good morning, Harry," I said, sitting up straight and trying to catch his attention as he passed our table. But instead of his usual friendly face, today his forehead was creased with worry lines, and his eyes were almost squinting.

He looked preoccupied. And he didn't seem eager to chat with us. "Everything okay?"

"You should have come in a little while ago," he said flatly. "Some kids were in here having an early breakfast. Your buddy Emmett was one of them."

"Emmett?" I said, nearly knocking over my brown cow.

Harry nodded, then looked nervously around the dining area. "It was him, all right. I told him I was surprised he was here so early. He usually comes in the evenings, during your shift after school."

Harry ran his hand over his chin. "He sat right here, in fact, at this table."

Emmett had been right here in Gerda's Diner? At our table?

Twenty-Three

$\mathcal{N}$EARLY SHOUTING, WE BEGAN BOMBARDING Harry with questions. *Who was he with? Where did he go? How did he seem? What did he say?*

Harry waved his hands to quiet us down.

"He seemed fine. He was here with my friend the Duke and some other kids. Three of them sat right here," Harry said, fumbling with his apron string. "I think they were working on some math problems . . . or puzzles, maybe? Smart kids, I hear."

And then Harry disappeared into the kitchen, saying something about poaching eggs.

Immediately I looked all around, frantically searching

for a sign of some sort. Emmett would have left behind a clue to tell me if he was okay or not. But where? And how? He wouldn't want the Duke to catch him.

I ran my hand along the underside of the table, feeling for a note—he could have stuck it there with bubble gum.

Nothing.

Then I felt all over the booth bench and in the crease where the back met the seat. Akiko and Mae checked theirs too. But all we found was some lint and a couple of pennies.

Akiko grabbed the menus and thumbed through them, looking for any sort of sign there. Mae poked around inside the napkin dispenser and unscrewed the salt and pepper shakers. Again, nothing. We shoved the stack of newspapers to the other side of the booth and even scanned the tabletop itself for some sort of hastily written message, but it was clean.

Then, like a silent snowflake, a sheet of white paper fluttered to the floor. It must have been tucked inside a newspaper. We sat stunned, watching as a customer stepped on it and left behind his shoe print.

"What's that?" rasped Akiko. "Could it be a note?"

She leaned out of the booth and picked it up. It was a simple sheet of white writing paper. We flipped it from one side to the other and saw that it was blank on both the front and the back. "Nothing here," she said, her voice heavy with frustration. "Maybe he meant to write something but ran out of time."

"Wait. Look a little closer," said Mac, taking the blank paper from Akiko's hand. "It looks stiff in some places, almost like there was a spill that dried."

She passed the paper to me, and right away I knew we had something. "I think this is a secret message!" I whispered, scrambling out of the booth as fast as I could. "Clever Emmett!"

I dashed through the diner to the kitchen, with Akiko and Mae trailing close behind. Thankfully, Harry was in the stockroom in the far back, so the three of us had a quick moment alone with the stove. And that was all we needed.

"You guys, make sure nobody comes over here," I said, my knees like wet noodles as I turned on the gas burner. I could hear Gerda at the cash register, ringing up a ticket.

Holding the paper above the flame—far enough away that I didn't set the paper on fire but close enough that the heat reached it—I held my breath and watched. And as if by magic, letters began to appear on the page:

SOS

HISSLER

DUKE

"How . . . ?" choked Akiko.

Mae was equally stunned, staring closely at the light brown words.

"What are you doing in here, pal?" came a voice from behind us. "Shall I put you to work making poached eggs, Josie? Your friends too?"

It was Harry! Akiko and Mae leapt toward him, blocking his view of the stove and Emmett's note.

"We're not doing anything, sir," squeaked Mae. "Akiko here was just curious about how the kitchen worked. So Josie took us on a tour."

"But we're done now," Akiko exclaimed, and I felt a swift kick to my ankle as she signaled me to get moving. "Your kitchen is fascinating!"

Just as I was about to step away—as I moved the lower part of the paper over the flame—one more word suddenly appeared beneath the others:

HARRY

I swooned as if the floor beneath me had opened up and I were falling.

I steadied myself, turned off the flame, then quickly folded the note and slipped it into the pocket of my dungarees. By the time we climbed back into our booth, my hands were trembling. Mae and Akiko were panting.

"How in the world did you know to do that?" marveled Mae.

"I knew Emmett would tell us something if he could," I

whispered, my mind still stunned by the thought of Harry's name on the note. Harry, my friend. Now Harry, as bad as the Duke and Mr. Hissler. I tried not to let on—I wasn't ready to share this news with Akiko and Mae.

"We were always passing notes back and forth at school," I went on, "usually with the letters scrambled so no one else could make sense of them." And tapping my pocket, I added, "I won't pull it out in case somebody sees it. But sometimes at lunch we'd write these kinds of notes."

"But where in the world do a couple of kids get invisible ink?" asked Akiko, still flabbergasted.

"We didn't have to use invisible ink from a bottle or anything," I explained. "We used milk from our lunches!"

Akiko smacked her forehead. "I should have remembered! I've read about this sort of thing, only not in a comic book." She sniffled, reaching into her bag and rummaging around for her hankie. "I read it in a magazine story about spy tricks!"

Mae gasped and touched her heart. "You don't think Emmett is the spy—"

"For Pete's sake, no," I said, snapping back to the moment. I tried to push thoughts of Harry's betrayal from my mind. "Emmett Shea is not a spy! He's just clever. Now, let's forget about how he did it. Let's figure out what he's telling us!"

We fell quiet as we thought hard about what Emmett's note said.

"*SOS*. That's the signal for distress," I began. "It's what ships use at sea when they're in danger."

"Next it said *Hissler*," whispered Mae, darting her eyes to the tables around us to make sure nobody was listening. "We'd already suspected he was up to no good, from Emmett's little sister yesterday. But now—"

"Now we know Hissler snatched Emmett," interrupted Akiko. "And with the Duke's name on that note too, he's just as big of a rat!"

And Harry right along with them.

Suddenly a plate appeared above us, held by a long arm that lowered it onto the center of our table. "For you, *Fräuleins*." I clutched my pocket where Emmett's note was tucked, the knowledge of Harry's betrayal searing my mind. "Pancakes. And eggs will be coming up in a few minutes. As I'm always telling Josie, pie just isn't enough for breakfast. Right, pal?"

"These smell delicious, Harry," said Akiko with an excited bounce. "You're a real gem!"

"Akiko's right," agreed Mae. "Thank you, sir. You're so kind."

Their compliments were like ice on a raw tooth. I felt myself jump.

"Delicious," I said, trying to sound as normal as possible despite the shouting that raged inside my head. On my feet now, I signaled for Mae and Akiko to get moving too. Immediately. "But we're in a hurry this morning. So we won't be taking anything more from you. Thanks—"

Trying to shape the last word, I could barely push it from my mouth.

"—pal."

Twenty-Four

$\mathcal{W}$E MADE OUR WAY OVER TO THE CARSON Building as quickly as we could, despite the complaints from Mae and Akiko about their empty stomachs. "Emmett is missing," I urged. "SOS is a distress signal. We can't just sit around sipping milkshakes and eating pie. We've got to find Mrs. B and Room Twelve."

The morning was hot and muggy already, and the summer sun was bright despite the early hour. When we reached the seventh floor, the smell of smoke and charred wood from yesterday's fire was strong. The hallway was blocked off with wooden barricades, and I could see crews cleaning up the damage.

"How are we going to find Mrs. B?" I asked, turning to gaze down the other hallways spreading out from the bank of elevators. I put my fingers to my mouth and whistled, which clearly embarrassed Mae and Akiko. "Hey, Astra might hear that! And he could lead us to her!"

We headed down another corridor, pressing our ears to doors along the way. But nothing seemed promising. We retraced our steps back to the elevators, then set out down a new hallway.

Finally we reached one doorway that gave us hope. We heard voices on the other side, the quiet drone of a radio program, and a bark. Though the brass numbers read 708, I had to remind myself that Room Twelve was a spy network, not a single location.

"Turn the knob," urged Mae nervously. "That's definitely her voice."

"You do it," insisted Akiko, adjusting the strap of her Hauntima bag. "What if that dog jumps on me? I hate dogs."

"I knew it!" said Mae, sounding as if she'd caught Akiko in the act of stealing a diamond. "You've got a thing against all animals!"

"If you had this nose and these allergies," Akiko protested, "you'd hate pets too. And flowers and perfume and dusty hiding places."

"Would you two can it?" I whispered. "You're going to get us thrown out of here. Now, let's find Mrs. B and ask her what we should do to rescue Emmett!"

With an exasperated huff, I knocked on the wooden door, wondering what we'd see on the other side. Would Mrs. B open the door in her pajamas? Nibbling on her breakfast toast? Would Astra be curled up on a cushion, still snoozing?

But when the door swung wide, we were definitely not looking at a sleepy scene. The room was teeming with activity as men and women rushed by, this way and that, and Mrs. B stood at the center of it, giving orders.

An official-looking secretary nodded his head like he recognized us. He stepped aside to let us in as Astra barked a greeting and trotted over. Mae scooped him up in her arms and rubbed her cheek on his curly hair. Akiko let out a little *pfft* noise and tried to ignore them.

"Josie, Mae, Akiko," Mrs. B said without even a hint of surprise. "We've been expecting you. Come right over. We have a great deal to discuss!"

An attendant wearing a radio headset ushered our trio into the wide, desk-filled room. Mrs. B carried a clipboard, and reading glasses dangled from a chain around her neck. Today, instead of a skirt, she wore trousers like me—and my favorite actress, Katharine Hepburn. I liked her immediately. I wasn't exactly sure how old she was. Maybe thirty? Or fifty? Anyone older than Kay looked the same to me. Her eyes were sharp and seemed to catch everything. Her brown hair was swept back from her face, and her mouth was set—not angry, but not exactly smiling. Again I noticed she walked with a limp. Her left leg seemed to be weaker than the other.

Busy workers bustled past in either direction, and Akiko, Mae, and I tried to step out of their way. The curtains were drawn together at the windows, and maps hung on all the walls. The room smelled of coffee and ink, and I could hear the tapping of typewriters as well as the sounds of news reports broadcasting on a few different radios. One announcer sounded British, another German, and even one Japanese. I counted maybe ten people moving about, but I suspected there were more.

"Sit down, young ladies, please," she said, waving toward a table along the far side of the room, where three wooden chairs sat waiting side by side. Astra jumped up to sit nearby. When I looked closer, I realized he had perched on the brown steamer trunk I'd carried on my shoulder yesterday.

I stared at it for a moment, wondering what was inside.

Mae slid silently into the seat closest to the dog. But Akiko made a commotion by dragging her chair away from the table, then sitting down and scooting it forward across the wooden floor with noisy hops. I took my place between the two of them and tried to look calm.

"You have made enormous sacrifices," began Mrs. B.

"What Room Twelve wants to know is, are you willing to go further?"

I gulped. Mae sat up a little straighter in her chair.

"Yesterday was spent protecting innocents from danger," she went on, "learning a bit about your various powers—"

"I only have one," interrupted Akiko, "and they each have two. I mean, if you don't count flying."

Mrs. B smiled patiently. "I do count flying. I count it very much. Don't you?"

Akiko stared at her for a few beats, then seemed to have second thoughts about any more complaining. Thankfully, she dropped the subject.

Still wearing a pleasant expression, Mrs. B looked just over our heads and signaled that papers or pencils or something be brought to our table. Moments later, I was stunned to see three milkshakes placed in front of us instead.

"How did you know Josie likes brown cows?" gasped Mae. "We never said anything about that!"

"And that Mae gets the chocolate malted," added Akiko. She sipped the drink in front of her, then sputtered, "And that I like egg creams?"

"We know a lot about you girls," answered Mrs. B casually, nodding again to the helpers. This time they slid plates of fresh-baked pie onto the table before us. "Josie, you prefer blueberry. Akiko likes apple. And for Mae, cherry."

The aroma of gooey fruit made my mouth pool with

saliva. I quickly wiped at my lips, hoping I didn't give Mrs. B the impression I was soft in the head or anything. After walking away from Harry's breakfast at the diner this morning, I was ready to eat. So I dove into my pie with gusto, and Akiko did too. But out of the corner of my right eye, I could see Mae, and she was sitting perfectly still.

"Mrs. Boudica, ma'am," she began, "my granny Crumpler says I shouldn't take food from strangers. Now, I'm not trying to be ill-mannered. But if you don't mind, could you tell us something about yourself? That way you won't be a stranger anymore, and I won't have to surrender my cherry pie and my malted."

Mae stared up at Mrs. B patiently, her big brown eyes as irresistible as a puppy's. Akiko's fork was halfway to her mouth, but she stopped it in midair. I did too, though it took more willpower than I wanted to admit.

"Well, I . . . er . . . ," began Mrs. B, a little flustered.

Mae blinked her thick lashes a few times, her fingers still threaded neatly together and waiting.

"I suppose I owe it to you girls to explain about myself and what's going on, especially since I know a good bit about each of you."

"That would be lovely," Mae said. And she finally reached for her fork. "Proceed."

Twenty-Five

HERE ARE LIMITS TO WHAT I CAN SAY, OF course," Mrs. B explained. "Not only for the security of Room Twelve, but for your own safety as well. You see, until yesterday Hank Hissler was a crucial part of our operation. If he were to catch up with you and discover that you knew too much, he might . . . well . . .

"Things could get unpleasant."

I shuddered. Mr. Hissler gave me the creeps. To think about Emmett in his clutches made my heart climb right up into my throat.

I had a hard time swallowing my pie.

"But what can you tell us?" pressed Akiko, as hungry

for more information as she was for her apple pie. "Who is Mr. Hissler? And who or what is Room Twelve?"

"Let's begin with Room Twelve," Mrs. B said patiently, her gaze steady as she studied us. "Our league of secret heroes is the most sophisticated military intelligence operation in the history of the world, to put it directly." She squared her shoulders just a bit as she spoke, which made her seem that much taller and grander.

"I've been a part of Room Twelve since the First World War—both my sister and I. We developed a few skills over the years: masters of disguise, you might say, and certain powers of the mind. And while my friends grew older and moved on, I never tired of the work. Nor did my sister, Dolores—we both loved it.

"Originally I started out as a code breaker, working under the leadership of my dear friend Elizebeth Friedman. You might come to know her. Lovely woman. Remarkable puzzler."

"We're puzzlers too," blurted Akiko, accidentally knocking her bag. A few newspapers spilled out. "Despite what Mr. Hissler thought of us."

Mrs. B nodded knowingly. "It may be that Hank Hissler rejected you," she said slyly. "Or it may be that we saw a better use for your talents. And we had just begun to suspect him of being a Nazi spy.

"Until the puzzlers went missing," she went on, pacing

the floor near our table, "we'd trusted him unconditionally. But now"—she crossed her arms and stared at our faces, her eyes moving from Akiko to me to Mae—"after what was done to the Stretcher, as well as the fire, well, now we know Mr. Hissler is no longer part of Room Twelve."

She paused for a moment, and I saw her jaw clench.

"Let me make it clear: Hank Hissler shall not get away with this."

The way she carried herself—chin out, shoulders square, spine straight—Mrs. B looked like she meant what she said. I wondered if this sister she talked about, Dolores, radiated the same sort of strength.

"And what about us?" Akiko asked, her eyes wary as she watched Astra approach her chair, tail wagging. He was just tall enough to rest his wiry head on her lap. Rather than scratch his ears, Akiko scowled at him before looking up. "You said something about a better use for us. Where do we fit in?"

Mrs. B reached a hand up and tugged on a cord dangling from a curtain rod behind her. She unfurled a white screen, then pointed at the helpers behind us. Suddenly a film projector whirred to life, and a movie played on the screen for us. It was a reel showing men coming and going from a downtown building. We watched in silence for a few minutes until a familiar figure crossed the screen.

"That's the Duke," I shouted, pointing with my fork. "We know him from Gerda's Diner!"

"And some of those thick necked ones are his hench-men," added Akiko. "They've been in the diner too."

"That lady on the right, with her hair in a bun," said Mae. "She's called Ursula. We've seen her with the Duke as well!"

Mrs. B nodded her approval.

"You girls were chosen for our project for a variety of reasons," she began. "The people you know, the abilities you have demonstrated as puzzlers, the traits you possess as unique individuals. But mostly, Room Twelve is interested in your participation because of what the three of you bring *together.*"

Akiko shook her head, her bobbed hair swinging. "I don't get it. The three of us have only known each other for twenty-four hours. What could we possibly bring to Room Twelve? Together, as you say?"

"Other than a love of superheroes," I added.

"Oh, and animals, too," offered Mae brightly.

"No," said Akiko, her eyes darting back down to Astra's furry face. "I hate dogs."

Mrs. B used a pointer to tap the screen and the images of the bad guys displayed up there. While Mae and I were paying close attention, I couldn't help but notice that Akiko, to the left of me, was not. She had pushed aside her milkshake and pie, and now she was hunching over the table to read one particular newspaper she'd brought from the diner. She had a notebook out too, and her pencil made a scratching sound as she jotted quick scribbles onto the paper.

"We have reason to believe Mr. Hissler, the Duke, and the Duke's men are planning to sabotage important sites around the city as part of a Nazi plot," Mrs. B said. She used a wooden pointer to note familiar buildings around town as the film reel played on. "And they plan to make these brilliant young boys—the puzzlers—help them do it."

Mae and I gasped, but still Akiko stayed focused on her newspaper.

"Our intelligence gathering here has also uncovered a location that appears to be one of their newest targets," she went on.

The image of a two-story building appeared, taking up the entire screen. Redbrick and stretching nearly a whole block, it looked vaguely familiar. "It seems that the government is working on a top secret military project," Mrs. B continued, "in the basement of the University of Pennsylvania's Moore School of Electrical Engineering."

Mae clutched my arm, and the hair on the back of my neck prickled.

Suddenly I knew exactly what building I was looking at: my cousin Kay's!

Twenty-Six

"KNOWN ONLY AS PROJECT PX, THEIR MISSION is to create the world's first electronic computer."

"Computer?" I blurted out, nearly shouting. "My cousin is a computer. What do you mean they're trying to make an electronic one? Do you mean a robot?"

"No, Josie, not a robot. They want to eliminate the human computers, since doing all the math calculations by hand takes too long. They want to build an electronic computing machine to handle the mathematical calculations—from what we've learned, with Project PX, what has taken their human computers *thirty hours* to calculate, a machine will solve in just *thirty seconds!*"

Mae wanted to know what anyone would do with an electronic computer. "What's so great about calculating problems that fast?"

Mrs. B reminded us that with the war on, every minute counted. "If we can calculate with greater speed and accuracy how bombs drop and missiles fire," she said, "then we will quickly bring an end to the war. And loved ones will return home to us that much sooner."

My heart felt like something was squeezing it. Between the worry for Kay and Emmett and the images in my mind of my father's plane flying over gunners in the Pacific, I couldn't breathe. Mae's eyes looked hopeful, and I knew she was thinking of her father driving an ambulance on the battlefields in Europe. The same went for Akiko and her worries for her brother coming home from the fighting. All of us had reasons—important reasons—to want this war over as fast as possible.

"Our spies have informed us," Mrs. B said slowly, "that this secret computer is being built in the basement of a building on the university's campus, at the Moore School of Electrical Engineering. You can find it at the corner of—"

"Walnut and Thirty-Third Street," I said, barely able to speak. "We know exactly where that is."

Suddenly Akiko leapt to her feet, sending her chair tumbling behind her.

"That's not where they're planning to strike first!" she

hollered, waving the newspaper page in the air. "Come look, Mrs. B. I think I've got something!"

Unfolding the front section, Akiko spread the newspaper out flat in the center of the table. We pressed in close to see what the fuss was all about.

"There are a bunch of words circled," she choked, trying to keep her excitement in check. "To anybody who looks at this, it seems like nothing. Just some doodling or messing around. Or like Emmett's coded laundry—something ordinary you see every day and barely give a second thought.

"But this newspaper," she went on, pausing for the rest of us to catch up, "is from the table where the Duke was sitting yesterday with this henchmen. So I don't think it's ordinary at all. Look what it says."

And she pointed to a headline and a story that ran in the far-left column of the page. There were a few words and letters circled in black pen. "'Twenty-seven,'" she said. "'Blow.' The letter *M*." Mrs. B jotted down each one.

"And over here, in this column," Mae said excitedly, "there are some more things marked. I see these words: 'Up.' 'Pier.' 'Ship.'" Mrs. B's pen scratched out the list.

My eyes raced across the page, tripping over circled letters and numbers as I went. "What does that word there say? 'Friday,' I think. The letter *P* right there, no? And there's 'Battle.'"

Mrs. B finished writing and turned the list around so

we could all see it. It matched word for word the list Akiko had just scribbled down. In silence, we stared.

Twenty-seven.
Blow.
M.
Up.
Pier.
Ship.
Friday.
P.
Battle.

We scanned the page for more markings. In a photo in the bottom-right corner, a woman held a drill in her hand, kerchief tied around her hair. She was one of the workers at the—

"'Naval Shipyard' is circled here," I said, a flutter of panic stirring in my chest. Suddenly my heart was a caged bird.

"And the number 'one' is underlined here," said Akiko, her eyes wide as she tapped the top of the page, "where the date is printed."

Mrs. B added them to our list, and in silence we tried to make sense of it all. The headlines and captions on the newspaper page began to swim, so I closed my eyes. But in their place, the words on our list blazed.

"Well, it makes perfect sense to me," announced Mae, squeezing my arm. The sweetness was gone from her face as she took a deep breath. "The Duke and his people—which includes Mr. Hissler—plan to blow up a battleship—"

"Friday at one twenty-seven p.m.," said Akiko, slurping down the last of her milkshake and setting it on the table with a noisy thud. "That's today! An hour away!"

I shook my head. Something wasn't quite right. All the marked words fit what Mae and Akiko were saying, except for one: "Pier."

"If we go at one twenty-seven today, we'll be too late." I ran my finger down Mrs. B's list. "I think they're going to try to blow up the battleship at one o'clock. And it's going to happen at Pier Twenty-Seven at the naval shipyard."

Mam! screamed a voice in my head. *No!*

Twenty-Seven

WE HAD LESS THAN AN HOUR.

If Room Twelve had been humming with activity earlier, now it seemed to be in full drive as people rushed past us in all directions. Only Mrs. B was standing still, the same cool, calm air about her as when I first saw her yesterday in front of Gerda's Diner.

"You say this paper comes from the Duke himself, is that right?" she asked Akiko, who nodded nervously. "Well, we can certainly count on a run-in with Hank Hissler, too. We should prepare for the worst."

I gulped. Knowing Mr. Hissler was capable of having the Stretcher vaporized yesterday and setting the fire that put all those innocent people in danger, I shuddered to think of what he might have in store today at the shipyard.

Mam's shift should have ended in the early morning. But what if she worked overtime? What if she was in Mr. Hissler's line of fire today? My knees gave out, and I sat back down in my chair between Mae and Akiko.

I imagined Emmett's note too, with Harry's name burned into my mind. I knew I should take a moment to tell the others, to stop everyone from darting around and make them listen. But I couldn't bring myself to utter Harry's name. How could I have been so naive to trust him? I wasn't as good a puzzler as I thought I was, if a spy like Harry was sitting right in front of me all this time. I winced at the memories—of Harry sharing photographs of his dogs, of Harry teaching me German songs.

Stupid girl. Maybe Toby Hunter was right all along.

"Astra, come!" ordered Mrs. B, grabbing her hat and slipping a light jacket over her shoulders. It hung all the way to her knees and fluttered behind her as she raced for the door. Astra was at her heels. "You girls hurry up too! We need to get to the shipyard—fast!"

Moments later, we were sitting at the back of the trolley, wind whipping our hair as we headed across town. Mrs. B's voice was steady as she gave us instructions.

"I am beginning to suspect that Hank Hissler is someone I once knew," she said, her voice so low, we had to lean in closer. Astra licked Akiko's cheek, which made her screech. She scrambled to her feet and switched places with Mae. Mrs. B waited, rubbing her weak leg like it was aching. "If this is the case, I've got to warn you about him:

"He angers quickly, and his attack is vicious," she began. "He will try to hypnotize you with his snakelike eyes. You must resist! You must look away! Whatever you do, don't let yourself be lulled into a trance. Be wary at all times!"

Akiko, Mae, and I nodded, looking at one another with bewildered expressions. I could hardly process what Mrs. B was telling us. Not only was she assuming we could turn into superheroes again, but she was telling us how to battle a villain!

"How do you know so much about Mr. Hissler?" asked Akiko.

"Let's just say if he's who I think he is," she said darkly, her hand clamped to her bad leg, "then we have a history together.

"Now pay attention. This is crucial: If you see his fangs bared and his eyes flash red, beware. That's the moment he's going to strike!"

Suddenly the trolley bell clanged, and we jumped to our feet. It was the stop for the shipyard. Mrs. B told us to go on ahead without her.

"My limp makes me walk too slowly, but don't worry," she reassured us. "I and the other Room Twelve agents will be scattered throughout the grounds. We'll do all we can to protcct you."

I heard Mae let out a little whimper. "All they can? What if that's not enough?"

I grabbed her arm, and Akiko's, too, and together we pushed through the crowds and hurried toward Pier 27. So many people were here—men, women, grandparents, little kids—to celebrate the completion of another battleship for the war effort. Even the workers took a break to wave out at the crowds from nearby ships: men operating enormous cranes and women holding flaming blowtorches.

"My mother is one of those," I said, nodding up toward a row of women wearing welding masks pushed back on their heads. I had to swallow before I could get the rest of my words out. "She works the night shift. I hope she's not here today for the celebration."

Mae and Akiko exchanged a look, then turned to me. "We'll try our best . . . ," they began. But I waved them off. Who knew what was ahead for any of us?

As we pushed on through the crowds, Mae warned that we should be on the lookout for anything suspicious. And for clues in the obvious places—like Emmett's laundry message. "The Duke, Mr. Hissler, their henchmen, even that blond computer Ursula could be here. Though they might be dressed in disguise."

I nodded. "You're exactly right. Their trick is to keep

things in plain sight. What might seem ordinary to us is something else entirely when it comes to them."

We hurried along as fast as we could through the throngs, past women in work clothes as well as those in everyday dresses. There were so many men wearing similar fedora hats that I felt like I was seeing Mr. Hissler at every turn. Kids were there too, some nibbling cotton candy, others eating peanuts.

"Those squirrels stole my snacks!" wailed one little boy as we passed a spilled bag of nuts. Bushy-tailed squirrels were filling their cheeks and making off with nearly the whole bag.

"There sure are a lot of rodents around here," said Mae as we passed under the arching gateway that read PIER 27. "Take a look at those rats! Have you ever seen them so big? Chicago has a lot of rats, but ours aren't nearly as fat as these!"

I looked to where Mae was pointing and felt the urge to run. I hated creepy things like rats and spiders. We had mice living in the walls of our apartment, and just the sound of them gnawed on my nerves. And these rats Mae had spotted, tucked behind a few crates on each side of the gangplank up to the battleship, were the stuff of nightmares. And as if their size and spindly tails weren't enough, they didn't seem to be afraid of anything either.

"Look at them," said Akiko, her nose crinkled in disgust. "You'd think with all the people around here, they'd get scared off. But look how they just sit there, staring at us with those glassy eyes. They're not scurrying away or anything!"

She jumped at them, stomping her foot on the wooden dock. "Yah! Shoo!"

But not one rat so much as flinched.

"Come on, Akiko," I said, my eyes scanning the crowd. "Let's keep looking for Hank Hissler and the others. We've got bigger rats to find, if you know what I mean."

The battleship was enormous as we gazed up at it from the pier. I looked ahead and saw two more wooden gangplanks angled up and leaning into the ship. Crews were busy carrying crates up and down the planks, and people both in uniform and out cheered from the ship's railing.

We pressed ahead, all three of us searching the crowd for familiar faces. As we passed the second gangplank, Mae spotted another rat and pinched her nose. "Disgusting!"

I turned away and nudged Akiko's shoulders, urging her to keep moving. But she wouldn't budge any farther.

"Look at that thing," she said, studying the revolting rodent. "Why doesn't it move? Or blink?"

This time Mae tried to shoo it away. But the rat sat immobile, its dead-looking eyes fixed on some spot in the distance. When I looked ahead, toward the next ramp angling up into the battleship, I strained to see whether more rats awaited us there. Just the thought of all these creepy vermin made my skin crawl.

But what I saw up ahead brought me right back to our job.

I squeezed Akiko's shoulder at the same time that I grabbed Mae's arm. "Take a look over there! Under the next ramp—near those boxes!" I whispered, though in my mind I was shouting. I shivered in disgust. "There's someone planting something there, and it looks round and furry and brown!"

"Rats!" Mae gasped in disbelief.

"The animal kind," Akiko added, "and the human kind too!"

I tugged them both under the nearest ramp to hide. Even though the idea of getting closer to these rats made my stomach turn somersaults, we had to find out what was happening.

"Go ahead, Akiko," I urged. "You're not afraid of anything. See if it's dead or alive."

"Are you kidding?" Akiko exclaimed, her eyes on me rather than on the rat. "I'm scared of plenty of things: my old piano teacher, bumblebees, dogs of any size, creamed corn—"

"Creamed corn?" shouted Mae. "Who in their right mind is afraid of corn, no matter how it's cooked? I've got to tell you, Josie, this kid is crazy! She's a few doughnuts short of a dozen!"

There was too much at stake for me to laugh, though at any other moment I probably would have been howling.

And it seemed clear that Akiko wasn't about to touch that rat to check on its current state of health.

"Okay, then," I said, turning to Mae. "You touch it. We know how much you love animals."

"Me?" she gasped, nearly shrieking. "I love animals, Josie, but not dead animals! You do it."

"Mae's right," Akiko agreed. "You don't seem afraid of much, Josie, so you should be the one to do it. You shouldn't be pressuring us to come in contact with those disease-infested creatures."

"Josie can make up her own mind, Akiko," said Mae, sounding a little exasperated. "She doesn't need you ordering her around."

"Well, she's been pretty bossy since we met," snapped Akiko, "so if she's making herself the leader of us three, then she'd better lead!"

This was becoming a regular thing, it seemed, finding myself caught in the middle between Akiko and Mae. And from the looks on their faces, I wasn't getting out of it. I turned to face the rat and squatted down on my knees. Its whiskers were long, and its black eyes were beady. My stomach lurched like I was on a swing set, and I had to squeeze my eyes shut for a moment just to keep my breakfast down.

"Give me a pencil or something, Akiko," I ordered. "Quickly! Whatever you've got in your bag!"

Despite some huffs and puffs, Akiko poked around in her Hauntima pouch, then passed me a pencil. With my hand trembling just a bit, I held the pencil out like a short stick. Then, leaning my body back as far as I could, I poked the rat.

It didn't flinch.

I poked it again.

Again, it stayed in the same crouch, beady black eyes unblinking.

"It's really dead," uttered Mae, a tremor in her voice.

"Not only is it dead," I whispered. "It's stuffed with something!"

With one last poke of Akiko's pencil, the stiff rat fell over onto its back. And that's when we saw what was packed inside:

"Dynamite!"

Twenty-Eight

SUDDENLY A SHADOW FELL ONTO THE dock's wooden slats. I looked up and was only a little surprised to see Harry standing there, his back to us as he looked nervously into the crowd.

I signaled for Mae and Akiko to be silent, edging backward until we could slip out the other side. And then we ran—partly to put distance between ourselves and the explosive rat. But also to find a place to talk.

"Why didn't we tell Harry what's happening?" Akiko said, her chest heaving as we came to a stop on the other side of a supply shed on the long pier. "If he's your friend, he should know what the Duke is up to, don't you think?"

"Dynamite! Exploding rats! This is getting serious," I panted. "I'll explain about Harry later, but for now we've got to do something to stop these bad guys! Something big, like we did yesterday!"

Waves lapped beneath us as we caught our breath. A few shrill seagulls complained about our sudden appearance at their hangout, sending up white feathers as they flapped and shrieked.

Mae suddenly gasped and pointed into the crowd about twenty feet away. Akiko turned and saw it too.

"Harry's not the only one we know here. Josie, I see your mom," whispered Mae, pointing into the crowd. "She's got your little brothers with her, and they're right there, waving those flags."

"And look who's right behind them," added Akiko, her voice a gravelly groan.

Finally I spotted them in the crush of people near the battleship—Mam looked happy, and Vinnie and Baby Lou were munching on pretzels and waving miniature versions of the Stars and Stripes. But when I looked just behind them, my stomach dropped like I was on a roller coaster.

Toby Hunter stood watching them, a sneer on his face.

"We've got to do something fast," Akiko reminded us, "before the Duke and his men act."

"Before anybody gets hurt," I added, my eyes still fixed on Toby leering at my family.

"But we don't have the pieces of the Stretcher's costume," Mae said, her expression frantic. "Our power came from the boots, mask, and cape!"

I shook my head and pulled my new friends closer, out of sight from any passersby on the dock. We stood so closely, I could feel the puffs of air from Akiko's heavy breathing and smell Mae's soapy fragrance. I caught the electrical thrumming now too, only faintly.

Then, the moment our shoulders pressed in tight to form a sort of triangle, the crackling current suddenly grew louder. I knew Mae and Akiko heard it too, because their eyes bulged in surprise.

"I don't think it was just the costume pieces that gave us our strength yesterday," I said, trying to be heard over the pulsing in our ears. "When it happened, I think there were other things too."

"Was it my Hauntima bag? Do you think it's magical? Like it has powers that can make us transform?" croaked Akiko. She raised her bag's wide strap in the middle of our triangle and began chanting. "Oh, magic bag—"

Mae rolled her eyes. "It wasn't your bag stuffed with junk!" she said, grabbing hold of Akiko's hand and letting the bag drop. "It was us. Like we talked about before—the three of us."

"Three to one," I added like a countdown. "Somehow connecting to each other and to the superheroes."

I reached in and clasped their hands, all of our fingers intertwining like the roots of a tree. Suddenly the familiar rush from yesterday whooshed in my ears, and the crackling electricity jolted through my body. The wind kicked up, lifting our hair, though it wasn't the hurricane we felt yesterday.

"But we're not transforming!" shouted Akiko. "Why isn't it happening this time?"

"It's not strong enough," answered Mae, though I could hardly hear her. "We're missing something." She flung one arm over my shoulder while her other clung to Akiko's hand and my own in the center of our triangle. Akiko and I did the same.

"Speak up," I shouted. "Say something that connects us to the superheroes!"

"Seriously?" asked Mae. "Josie, that doesn't seem—"

"My mask!" Akiko blurted. "I want to protect innocent people like Hopscotch in her awesome mask! And like Hauntima with all her powers!"

And suddenly a faint beam of golden light shot into the air from our clasped hands. The thrumming was louder than ever, and the same electrical surge I'd felt back at the Carson Building rushed through my body.

"Your turn now, Mae!" hollered Akiko. "Go!"

"Those boots!" she called. "I want to wear those boots again so I can fight for justice like Nova the Sunchaser and the Palomino!"

The light grew more dazzling, shooting higher into the air as the wind kicked up. Our hair whipped in all directions now, and from what I could tell of Akiko and Mae, the electrical charge was pulsing through their veins too.

"And I want to wear the cape again," I hollered, "and do good like brave and bold Zenobia!"

In a flash, the golden light burst brighter than before and began to spin faster and faster until it was swirling around us. I had to squint as the wind funneled up like a tornado, whipping our hair, our clothes, even our shouts. I felt our bodies lift off the ground just like yesterday, and we hovered suspended in the air a few feet above the dock. Just when I thought I couldn't take it anymore, the pulsing in my ears nearly deafening, suddenly I saw a burst of green, then violet, then orange.

And when we fell apart from one another, we tumbled backward and collapsed onto the dock, transformed.

"We did it." Akiko wheezed as she propped herself up on her elbows. "I can't believe you were right!"

"Thanks for the boost of confidence," I replied. "I can't believe you're orange!"

Akiko's fiery orange cape blazed brightly against the drab gray of the shipyard, and Mae's shimmering purple one snapped in the wind like the flags on the battleship behind us. As I scrambled to my feet, I grabbed hold of the emerald cape that fell from my shoulders and ran my hands over its silky material.

I kicked out a foot and gazed down at my incredible green boots. Again, we were clad in the same black bodysuits as yesterday, our masks and boots matching our magnificent capes.

"We can do this," I whispered, turning to Mae and Akiko. But really, I said those words to convince myself. My hands were trembling as I thought of Emmett. Who would be next? Kay? And what about Mam and my brothers? I'd keep Toby Hunter away from them, no matter the cost.

"The time to act is now," agreed Akiko, her voice low and serious.

"We can't wait for one more person to get hurt," added Mae.

Throwing my arms above my head, I leapt into the air. It wasn't as graceful as diving into a pool, but who cared? The wind lifted my cape and my body, and I was flying again. It was the best feeling in the world, and I could hear Mae and Akiko soaring with me on either side.

"Those dynamite-stuffed rats may be dead, but they sure tell us a lot," I shouted. "Mr. Hissler and the Duke must be planning to carry out their terrible scheme!"

"But how can we find them in a crowd this big?" wondered Akiko. "It's nearly impossible to tell one person from the next up here."

Mae pointed to the clock tower we'd passed as we came in. "It's nearly one o'clock," she warned. "We only have a few minutes to stop them, Josie!"

"Don't use her name," shouted Akiko. "Nobody can know our true identities. It's too dangerous—for us and for our families!"

"Now we're really like the superheroes." I grinned. "Just think of Zenobia and the Palomino. Nobody ever found out their real identities either!"

Suddenly the crowd below us erupted into shouting. From where we flew above them, we could see the commotion. Along the edge of the pier closest to the battleship, three different men were spilling canisters of a clear liquid.

"That must be gasoline," Akiko said. "I bet they're going to light a match and set it on fire."

Mae's voice was full of outrage. "And the flames will race to where the dead rats are waiting. With all the dynamite stuffed inside them, those rats are going to explode!"

"This whole place is going to be blown to bits!" I said frantically. "What should we do? Where do we begin?"

"Remember what I told you," came an eerie voice. "Whatever strength you need dwells within you."

It was Hauntima—or rather her ghost form! Thank goodness she was back!

"This villain is so vile," Hauntima said angrily. "He wants to harm hundreds of innocents! We must stop him.

"Hauntima wills it!"

I circled closer around her form, feeling suddenly both inspired and a little scared at the sight of her angry skulled face. "If I concentrate hard enough," I said haltingly, "do you think my power of telekinesis might be able to knock the gas cans from their hands?"

Hauntima nodded her approval, then turned to Mae.

"Scan the crowd," she said, her expression angry. "Use your telepathy power to find the fiend!"

"Right," Mae answered, "then maybe I can catch their thoughts and find out what else they're plotting to do!"

And finally, Hauntima gazed over at Akiko. "The stuffed rats," she began spookily, pointing with one nearly transparent arm. "Can you think of something to transform into? Something that will knock them into the wa—"

But Akiko was too eager to find out more about Hauntima to focus on the current danger. She fired off questions like she was a newspaper reporter.

"Why are you a ghost? Where have you been since you disappeared? Where are the other missing superheroes?"

I wanted answers too, but this was no time for an interview. We needed to act!

"Hey, Orange!" I hollered in Akiko's direction, careful not to say her name. "Get moving already, would ya? Leave the chitchat for later!"

Mae, Akiko, and I took off in different directions. I

hovered in the air above the battleship and studied the ramps leading on board. I tried to push the panicky fear about Mam and my brothers aside. But thoughts of Emmett in Mr. Hissler's clutches made me nearly dizzy with worry. Focusing my mind on the gas canisters, I counted them— *one, two, three.* I flicked my head to the side—*once, twice, three times.* But instead of popping out of the bad guys' hands, the canisters just knocked into their noses.

"Ouch!" I heard one of them holler to another lunk-head. "What'd you that for?"

I flew a quick circle, then hovered over them again. I focused my eyes on those gasoline cans, this time using all my powers of concentration. Again I flicked my head—*once, twice, three times.* I heard three loud bangs and saw the metal canisters crash to the ground behind them.

I punched a fist into the air. It felt good to finally be useful!

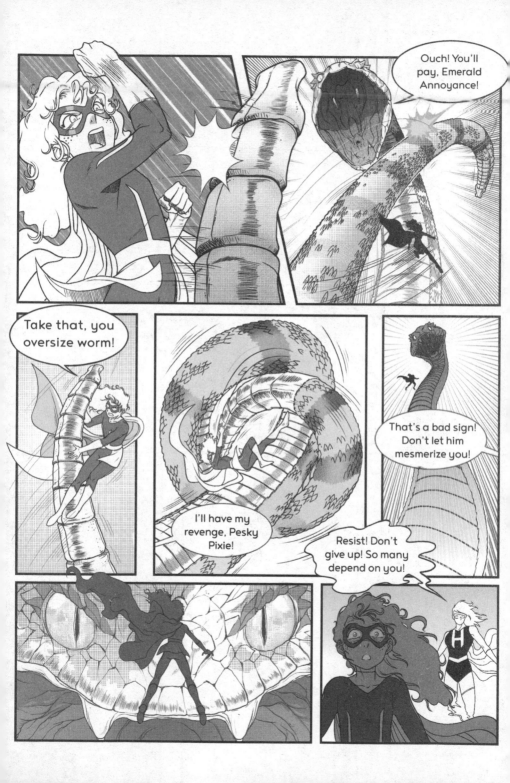

Thirty

E FLEW OVER THE CITY FOR WHAT MUST have been hours, searching for Akiko down every street, sidewalk, and alley we could find. Each time we spotted even a hint of orange below us, Mae and I swooped closer to investigate.

"She must be unconscious," Mae said, "or else I'd be able to use telepathy to read her mind and learn what's happening."

"The Hisser must have whisked her away to his hiding spot," I said, feeling heavy with worry. "We've got to figure out where that is. I bet he's locked up Emmett there too!"

I was mindful of the sun dipping below the horizon to

our right. With the war on, the city was under a blackout order. Businesses, homes, streets—everyone had to turn out their lights for the night. With each passing minute, our chances of finding Akiko—and Emmett—were slipping away.

"And we've got to find the Hisser before he strikes again," Mae said, her usually upbeat voice replaced by a quiet sadness. "He could be anywhere."

We flew on in silence, the only sounds the wind whipping in our ears and our capes snapping behind us.

"Let's go over it all one more time," I began, though I could tell Mae was growing frustrated. "Where else would the Hisser plan to strike? We've flown past the ammunition factory three times, past Independence Hall and the Liberty Bell twice, and we've even checked on the battleship again. There's no sign of the Hisser or the Duke."

"At least your cousin Kay's building has been quiet," Mae added, "all four times we checked on it. I don't think the Hisser knows about Project PX and what the human computers are doing there. At least not yet."

I thought about that blond woman Ursula, whom we'd seen with the Duke. What secrets had she already spilled? And what had they both passed along to the Hisser?

My heart was in my throat, making it hard to speak anymore. There was evil moving about the city, evil that could hurt hundreds if not thousands of innocent lives—including the people I loved.

And we had no idea how to stop it.

Where was Mrs. B when we needed her? And why did Hauntima have to leave us? I tried to work out the answers on my own, but I was growing angrier by the minute. We were just kids! We could use some help from real superheroes like Hopscotch or Nova the Sunchaser, not just some ghost. Where was Zenobia? And her sister, the Palomino?

Had they all abandoned us? Had they really quit?

"Come on," I said, adjusting my mask and plunging toward the rooftop of a building below. "Let's go back to my apartment before our arms fall off. We need to sit down and think things through."

Mae agreed, saying she'd never felt more tired. "But I know I won't sleep tonight. Not when we need to solve the most important puzzle of our lives."

We landed on the roof of my building and transformed back to our usual selves in the snap of a finger. Slipping down the fire escape, we managed to climb through an open window and into the kitchen of my apartment without getting caught.

The radio was playing as Mam emerged from the bathroom, tying a scarf around her hair. She greeted us as she passed by, rushing to get ready before heading off to another night shift at the shipyard factory.

"I didn't hear you girls come in," she said, throwing a curious look at the usually squeaky apartment door. But thankfully, she was too busy to ask questions, focusing instead on the clutter we kids had left everywhere. "Where's your friend? The sniffly one?"

"Akiko?" I asked, trying to sound cheerful though my heart was breaking. I winced at the thought of her out there in the city somewhere, like Emmett, in the clutches of the horrible Hisser. "She couldn't come—she got held up a bit. But I was hoping Mae here could spend the night again. We're making real progress on that puzzler research.

"If it's okay with Mae's grandmother, can she stay?"

Mam gave me a questioning look.

"Let's go down and call her together, shall we?" she asked. "Boys, I'm making a telephone call downstairs at the phone booth in Mr. Hunter's barbershop. I'll be right back."

Mae and I trailed after Mam, making silent faces and wild gestures about what Granny Crumpler would say when she heard from my mother. Mae tugged on her curls, whispering that a loud "NO!" was coming. I held out hope that my mother might win her over. What else could we do?

While Mam stood in the telephone booth and talked to Mae's granny, Mae and I found ourselves face-to-face with the horrible Toby Hunter's equally horrible father. He was a whiskered version of his bullying son. Mr. Hunter ran his barbershop on the first floor and lived above it in the apartment on the second floor, right below ours.

"Haven't seen you in a while, Miss O'Malley," he said, and I knew he called me that because he couldn't remember my first name. "But I've heard a good deal of you. You walk like an elephant. You and your mother and your brothers, too. A whole pride of elephants."

"Herd," said Mae softly. "Sir. Lions travel in a pride, elephants in a herd, hummingbirds in a charm."

Mr. Hunter glared at us.

"My son knows all that," he began. "He's the smartest kid in his class. Toughest, too, like his old man."

Immediately my mind jumped to Toby, his team of bullies, and the stolen bikes. I winked at Mae and started a new conversation, making sure my voice was loud enough for Mr. Hunter to catch every word.

"Oh, Mae, did you hear? They've got extra patrolmen out to catch those bike thieves. Seems the chief of police's kids had their bikes stolen just last week. Can you imagine the trouble somebody's going to face when they get caught with all those stolen bicycles?"

"It's never a good idea to steal from the police, is it?" said Mae with a nervous chuckle. "That doesn't sound too bright."

I peeked over at Mr. Hunter, who was staring at me and cleaning his scissors. I wasn't sure exactly what my plan was to get Toby to return my brothers' bikes, but I figured it probably took big talk to intimidate a bully.

Suddenly Mam was pushing out of the phone booth and beaming at Mae. "Your delightful grandmother says yes," she said. "And she knows my dear friend Millie, who's a librarian across town. What a small world."

As we climbed back up the stairs, Mam was saying something about Spam hash for dinner and bedtimes for the boys. I could barely focus on any of it. My thoughts were on Akiko and Emmett and where they would sleep tonight.

"Pardon me, Mrs. O'Malley," said Mae, timidly taking a step forward. "I apologize for being so bold. But we were hoping to visit with Cousin Kay. Do you happen to know what time she's coming home?"

Mam smiled and shook her head, stepping into our apartment. "I'd love to catch up with Kay myself, dear. But I don't think we'll see much of her this week. She said something about a new project she's been placed on. Called it important, I think."

Project PX.

Mae and I looked at each other knowingly.

"Two things before I go," Mam said, taking both my hands in hers. "First is that the boys and I saw the most remarkable thing today at the shipyard—we were at the dedication ceremony for the new battleship. And three superheroes were fighting with what seemed to be a super-villain, a real viper. It's been years! Your brothers can tell you about it. But, Josie"—and she looked deep into my eyes with that familiar sadness—"that terrible viper. I can't bear to think of any harm coming to you or the boys. Please. Be safe. No trouble."

And she kissed my forehead.

"I get it, Mam. I really do," I said, choking the words out. I wanted to move us off the topic of superheroes as quickly as I could. "What else? You said two things."

"Right," she continued. "Mr. Hunter's son stopped by an hour or so ago. That Toby boy. He said something about wanting to talk to you. Vinnie and Baby Lou looked upset by the mere sight of him. Is everything okay?"

Panic surged through my veins, and I couldn't help but look at my little brothers. Toby had been here, inside our apartment? He'd been acting like he knew about the telegram. What if he knew Mam's secret? *Our* secret? I wanted to grab my family and flee, to someplace where we wouldn't have to deal with mean people.

"Thanks," I replied, keeping my voice as calm as I could. "I'll look for him."

With one more quick hug and kisses blown to my little brothers in the living room, Mam left for work.

"We're playing a game," announced Baby Lou as he bounced over to us. "I'm winning, but I think Vinnie might be letting me. I can tell he'th paying attention to the radio report more than our Parcheethi."

"Mae and I are going to sit down for some dinner. Want

to join us?" I said, knowing he and Vinnie would stay as far away from Spam hash as they possibly could.

Baby Lou scampered back to the living room and tackled Vinnie. And as Mae and I headed for the kitchen, we could hear them wrestling and knocking into the coffee table.

"We don't have to do this," I said as I scooped Mam's dinner onto our plates. Though the Spam smelled disgusting, I was too hungry and tired to care. "We're just kids, after all. We could leave this work to somebody else—somebody bigger or older or . . ."

I let my voice trail off. Because I knew quitting wasn't the right option.

When the world needs a hero, that's what you become. Isn't this what Mam was always telling us?

"I've been thinking about it," said Mae, politely moving the hash around her plate with her fork. "When things get really difficult, that's when it's most important to work harder—and smarter. That's when it matters most of all."

"Did your granny Crumpler teach you that?" I asked in between bites.

Mae shook her head. "No. That one's mine. I don't like to walk away from a fight. I don't go looking for them, that's for sure. But when the time comes, I'm not one to back down."

We sat quietly and stared at our plates. My mind was focused on Akiko and Emmett, and I was sure Mae's was just the same. She picked at her food but didn't take a bite. I couldn't blame her. I lifted a mound of the Spam hash toward my nose, but the smell made me drop my fork and push my plate to the side. I lost my appetite.

The radio in the dining room was always playing these days, so I'd hardly paid attention to it earlier. But now the latest report from Europe reached our ears. It was bad news.

"Nazi troops launched a deadly attack today. Explosions could be heard for miles around as Allied American and British forces suffered heavy losses. . . ."

Heavy losses. That meant soldiers were wounded or dying. Immediately I thought of my dad and felt a sob catch in my throat. I looked across at Mae and saw her bite her lip. I knew she was worrying about her father too. For all of us sitting by our radios, in houses and apartments across the country and around the world, loved ones were fighting on beaches and battlefields a thousand miles away from us. But they were never ever far from our thoughts.

Thirty-One

"JOSIE, WILL YOU TELL US A BEDTIME STORY?" came Vinnie's voice from behind my chair. "We're tired from swimming and basketball after school."

"I finally beat Vinnie at Parcheethi," said Baby Lou with a yawn. "That tired me out too."

I excused myself from the kitchen, asking Mae to put a kettle on for the two of us once I returned. Then I led my little brothers back to the living room to lie down for the night.

Pushing aside the mound of comic books—*Hauntima, Hopscotch, Nova the Sunchaser,* and an old one featuring Zenobia, the Palomino, and the Palomino's smart wolflike sidekick called Star—I let them fall onto the wooden floor. Maybe it was true what Mae said yesterday, that superheroes could be found only in comic books and statues now. Not in real life anymore.

I glanced out the window, wishing that Hauntima's ghost would suddenly make an appearance on the neighboring apartment's rooftop. Then I would ask her about Emmett and Akiko and whether they were going to be all right, and about the Stretcher and what happened to him.

"This time tell us about Daddy and the Battle of Midway," Vinnie began, bringing me back to the living room sofa and bedtime. "And start it the morning the planes came."

"Yeth, when Daddy thounded the alarmth that the Japanethe bomberth were coming," chimed Lou. He rubbed his eyes with his fists, his hands still chubby with baby fat.

My stories were always full of dangerous deeds and heroic acts, pulled right from the pages of our comic books. But instead of superheroes populating these adventures, I'd tell Vinnie and Baby Lou that it was our dad performing the feats of daring. My brothers would fall asleep wearing smiles, snuggled in together on the living room couch.

Since our apartment was so small, Kay and I shared one bedroom, and Mam got her own. Which meant my brothers took the sofa. But rather than sleep end to end, they insisted on smashing together like two slices of bread. This way if either of them woke up from a nightmare, the other was close by.

"When is Daddy coming back?" asked Vinnie. "That bully Toby Hunter stopped by today. He was asking me and Lou about Daddy."

I closed my eyes and caught my breath. Like Mam, there was only so much more I could take. I counted to five, then looked at Vinnie and Baby Lou.

"Don't listen to anything Toby Hunter says," I told them, trying to keep the anger out of my voice. "Daddy would come to you in a heartbeat if he could. You know that, right?"

Vinnie nodded and picked at the green blanket.

"I don't feel like telling stories about Daddy and his battles tonight," I said, the words tight in my throat. "I'm done with those for a while. Instead I want to tell you about Grandpa O'Malley and a stolen motorcar."

"Why won't you tell us about Daddy fighting the dive-bombers?" urged Vinnie, his hair dark against the white pillow. "That's the story we want."

"I mith Daddy," complained Baby Lou in a hoarse whisper. "Pleathe, Jothie."

I stared down at the two of them, their heads nearly touching on the pillow, messy hair blending together. A warm breeze lifted the curtain beside us, but I shivered anyway. Sometimes it was hard to remember how it was before our father went off to war. My stories brought Dad back home. And made him a hero.

But I just couldn't do it tonight. I ignored their badgering and began an old family story of our grandfather and a motorcar that went missing. Curling up with a cushion on the floor beside them, I could see Mae in the yellow light of the kitchen. She sat at the table quietly reading the newspaper and ignoring the Spam hash.

I went on with the familiar tale, but Vinnie and Baby Lou stopped my story before I could even get to the best part. Tears were in Lou's eyes as Vinnie made one last plea for a story about our father's brave deeds.

"Please, Josie. If you won't tell us about the Battle of Midway, at least tell us the one about Daddy at Pearl Harbor."

"I told you that one last night." I rolled my eyes and let out an exasperated sigh. They already knew every detail of that story: how Japan's early morning attack drew America into World War II, how more than two thousand people had lost their lives and more than one thousand were wounded. President Roosevelt's "date which will live in infamy" speech was seared into our memories.

But it was our father they wanted more than anything. When I told them about his heroics, stories about how he'd saved the men around him and faced down danger without flinching, they took comfort. "He'd be with us if he could," Vinnie liked to say, "but he's saving other soldiers."

My stories made Dad's absence easier for them.

"Okay, okay, I'll tell you this time," I whispered, glancing again toward the kitchen to make sure Mae was still at the table. "But remember—"

"We know," Vinnie said impatiently. "Don't talk about it in front of anybody else. Because it makes them miss Dad too."

"Now thtart it like you alwayth do, Jothie," urged Baby Lou, patting my arm affectionately. "Daddy was having hith breakfatht—two poached eggth, a thlice of toatht, and black coffee, jutht like any other morning—when he heard . . ."

" . . . when he heard the low drone of airplanes in the distance," I picked up. "Suddenly the air-raid sirens began to blare, warning the men on his battleship that an attack was underway. Still wearing his pajamas, Daddy raced upstairs as enemy fire strafed the quarterdeck. Dodging bullets and bombs, he rushed to an injured crewmate and threw him over his shoulder. Daddy carried him to safety, then ran back to help the others. . . ."

"Can you speak a little louder?" came Mae's soft voice. She was standing at the edge of the living room now. She leaned quietly against the doorframe and urged me to go on. "I want to hear it too."

I stared at her, blinking for a moment.

This was our story. It belonged to Vinnie, Baby Lou, and me. I didn't want to share it with anyone else, especially not Mae or even Akiko if she were here. All of us wanted to protect our families from hurt and harm. This was my way of protecting my little brothers.

"Go on, Josie," said Vinnie, his voice pleading in the blue darkness. "Daddy went back to help the others. . . ."

But I couldn't.

"Mae," I whispered. "I'll meet you in the kitchen once I've tucked them in. But until then, would you mind giving us a few minutes?"

Thirty-Two

WHEN I RETURNED TO THE KITCHEN A WHILE later, the radio was still broadcasting the same terrible news about Allied losses in Europe. I took a seat at the table and sipped my cold tea as Mae nibbled on a shortbread cookie.

After a while she spoke. "You don't trust too many people, do you?"

I shrugged. What could I say? The war made it hard to believe—in people and in ideas.

"Well, if I'm supposed to fly around beside you," she said, "risking my life and fighting bad guys, I need to trust you. And you need to trust me. So that means we have to learn a little bit about each other."

I got up and put the kettle on for more tea. I made sure my back was turned to Mae, so she couldn't see my face. I was afraid my eyes would give away my sadness.

"I can't, Mae" was all I could get out. "I'll share things with you, but not now."

I stood at the stove until the kettle began to whistle. After pouring a cup for Mae and then myself, I took my seat again. Mae gave me a weak smile that told me she could wait. I knew I'd probably hurt her feelings. But her patience made me like her even more.

We stared at our teacups, lost in our own thoughts as the radio went on about casualties and bombing attacks.

"You can listen to depressing news like that all day," came a gravelly voice at the window, "but if you really want to stop this evil, you've got to get back out there and fight!"

And then two scrawny legs poked into the room from the fire escape.

"Akiko!" I half whispered and half shouted, astonished by the sight of her. "You're safe!"

Mae jumped to her feet too, and we both rushed to help her climb inside, throwing our arms around the most wonderful, most cranky asthmatic in the world! And we squeezed tight despite her complaints about too much sentimental fussing.

"Let a kid breathe, would ya?" Akiko choked, though I could tell she was just as happy to see us again.

"We were so worried," Mae said, plucking a few leaves

from Akiko's hair. "Sit down and tell us everything that happened."

"And how you got away from the Hisser," I said. I pulled out a chair for her to sit down at the table and grabbed the Spam hash and an extra plate. "Did you outsmart him?" Then, dropping to a whisper so Vinnie and Baby Lou wouldn't hear, "Did you shape-shift?"

"As a matter of fact," Akiko said, looking annoyed, "there's a little detail you both should know about. I think when one of us transforms from caped hero back to everyday kid, it happens to all of us. At the exact same time!"

Mae squinted. She looked doubtfully at Akiko.

"Really?" she asked. "What makes you think that?"

"The fact that one minute I was just flying along, having escaped the Hisser's grasp," she said a little huffily, "and the next I was falling out of the sky!"

I knocked over the container of milk for the tea, and Mae dropped into her chair with a thud. "What?" we both exclaimed. "Are you okay?"

"I'm fine," Akiko explained, nudging away the plate of Spam. "Luckily, I was flying pretty low, so a weeping willow broke my fall. But I had to walk the rest of the way here. I'm just glad I remembered how to find your apartment. Your front door's buzzer is broken, by the way," she added, pointing at the fire escape. "Which is why I climbed that."

I was glad she remembered how to find it too! What if

we'd transformed earlier, while she was still in the Hisser's clutches? That could have been a disaster.

"So how did you get away from that horrible snake man?" asked Mae, looking a little shaken by Akiko's news. "Did you shape-shift into a leaf and blow away? Into a puddle and drip out of his hands? Into a squirrel and race up a tree?"

"No, no, and no, though I like all of those ideas," Akiko said, sounding a little mysterious. Then she leaned in close and whispered, "I discovered another superpower. And let's just say it makes having allergies a lot less annoying."

Mae and I named every power we could think of: invisibility, X-ray vision, elasticity, superspeed, superhearing . . . The list went on and on. But Akiko shook her head at every one.

"Here's a clue: In some cultures, fried snake is a delicious treat."

Mae and I raised our eyebrows, clearly stumped.

"*Fried*," Akiko said proudly, "as in, I can control fire! Though maybe 'control' is too strong a word. The fire seems to happen when I sneeze. So that's how I got away."

Pyrokinesis. Thank goodness for Akiko's allergies.

Mae and I were full of questions. About Emmett, where the Hisser's hideaway was, who was there with him, what Akiko saw and heard and understood, and if she'd come across the other puzzlers.

Just thinking about Emmett sleeping away from his home tonight made my heart sink. He must have been so scared. And his poor little sister, Audrey, too—all I ever thought about was protecting my family from the bad things in this world. I shot a look into the living room, grateful to know that Vinnie and Baby Lou were safe.

But Kay? A shudder of fear whispered down my spine as I thought of Kay and the other human computers. I tried to remind myself that she was okay. *Please don't worry*, she'd told us. *Very few people know about this place. We're safe.*

"What do you think he'll do next?" I asked, dreading Akiko's answer. "Mrs. B mentioned the computers. Do you think he knows about Kay and the other women?"

Akiko shook her head. "The Hisser is plenty smart," she said, "but I didn't hear anybody mention the word 'computer.' He did tell the Duke that he'd overheard one of the Caped Kiddies, as he calls us, give away a secret. But I have no idea what he thinks he heard. None of us would have given anything away. Right?"

My breathing seized up in my chest. Did I let something slip about my cousin? About the Moore School? What if I'd messed up again, like I'd done with Emmett and my talk of milkshakes?

"So I think we can assume Kay and the others are safe for now," Akiko went on. "When it comes to the Moore School and their secret project, the Hisser didn't appear to have a clue."

They're safe, I told myself, my teacup rattling in its saucer as I set it on the table. *They're fine*, I repeated again and again in my mind. *They're inside the Moore School, safe and fine, and nobody knows what they're up to.*

"Josie, your hands are shaking," said Mae gently. "What's got you so afraid?"

I closed my eyes. How could I even begin to tell them about my mom and her secret? Our secret. And how much it made my bones ache with sadness. Mae talked of trust. But I didn't want to betray Mam's trust. And to think that Toby Hunter might be the only other person who knew our secret made me feel furious and frightened.

Powerless.

"I worry about my family too, Josie. When we had to leave our home in San Francisco for the internment camp, I thought it sounded like a summer camp—an adventure. But it's nothing like that. With summer camp, you get to go back home after a couple weeks. My family has been there for more than a year—my grandfather even died there. They said it was pneumonia, but I know it was a broken heart.

"After he died, the government let my parents send me here to be with my cousins. And Tommy, he signed up to go fight—despite what happened to us. My grandparents, my parents, my brother, and me, we didn't do anything wrong. We were locked up in prison just for being Japanese. It makes my heart hurt so much, sometimes I can't eat, can't sleep."

I tried to picture it in my head. I'd read about those

camps. And even worse, the ones in Germany where the Nazis were rounding up Jewish people.

Akiko's breathing was fast, and she stared at her hands on the table.

"We're all human beings. Why do people treat each other this way?"

She took a sip of tea, then wiped at one of her eyes. Only this time, I knew it wasn't allergies to blame.

"I can't sleep sometimes either because of all the worrying," said Mae, her voice barely above a whisper. "Every time I hear a report on the radio, I picture my daddy on the front lines and wonder if he's ever coming home. I don't like to use the word 'hate.' But I hate this war. I hate the guns and the bombs and the fighting.

"I just want my dad."

I took a breath and tried to stop the sob that was building in my chest. I knew that if I tried to utter a single word, I might never stop crying. So I reached my hands out to each of theirs and squeezed. It was all I could do.

"So, do you want to hear what happened to me or not?" said Akiko, her voice returning to its usual strength. I knew she wanted to change the subject as much as I did.

"Yes, tell us what happened," urged Mae, scooting her chair closer. I nodded and moved mine in too. Akiko gulped more tea, then perched on the edge of her seat.

"When I came to, I wasn't sure where I was. It seemed

like an ordinary office, like Room Twelve with Mrs. B. Only, I could hear the deep foghorns of ships going by, so it must have been near the waterfront. Maybe close to the naval shipyard, I figured.

"Emmett and the other puzzlers—I think I counted five of them in all—were kept busy at tables. They couldn't escape or anything because a couple of thick-necked goons were keeping watch. Emmett and the others were wearing headsets over their ears, connected to radios, and they had to write down what was being said. It seemed to me like they were being used to crack coded messages, but I'm not certain."

"How did Emmett seem?" I asked. "W-was he all right?"

Akiko nodded, but her face looked concerned.

"He passed me a note. I haven't had time to try to make sense of it," she said, pulling a scrap of paper from her Hauntima bag and laying it out on the table between us. "I think it's written in one of your secret codes."

In block letters, it read:

GARDEN RANGED GANDER!

EXPORT JACKY P.

HEN WOKS.

Just then Vinnie slipped into the kitchen and over to the pantry. He tucked what was left of the Lorna Doone cookies into his pajama top and tried to sneak past us unnoticed.

"Where are you going with those cookies?" I asked, sticking my arm out to block his way. "Those are for my friends and me."

Vinnie craned his neck and asked what we were talking about so secretively. But I ushered him into the hallway before he could catch sight of Emmett's latest note.

"Listen, Vinnie, I have a new comic book hidden somewhere in the apartment," I whispered, careful not to wake Baby Lou. He perked up his ears, since one mention of the word "new" grabbed everybody's attention. With the war on, new things were hard to come by.

"If you give me what's left of the cookies," I continued, "I'll let you have that comic book."

Vinnie stared hard into my eyes. He was getting too smart for my usual tricks. "What are you all talking about that's so important? It must be good if you're willing to give up a comic book for it."

I dashed into my bedroom and reached under my mattress. As much as I wanted to keep the latest *Miss Smash* for myself, I knew this was the best way to bribe my brother. Akiko, Mae, and I were still starving, and we had a long night of puzzling ahead. Spam hash was not going to get us through, but my favorite cookies certainly could.

I quickly tucked Vinnie back under the green blanket beside Lou, leaving a dim light on in the hallway so he could sleepily read my comic book. This way, Mae,

Akiko, and I could focus on Emmett's message.

"I can tell right away that the first line is something important," said Mae as I set down three glasses of milk for cookie dipping. "Because those are three different words, but they all use the same letters."

I stared at the note:

GARDEN RANGED GANDER!

And right away I knew what Emmett was saying: "Danger! Those words all spell 'danger'!"

One line down, two more to go. I could feel sweat break out under my arms and along my neck.

"And the middle line, with that letter *X*," Mae said, running her finger beneath the words:

EXPORT JACKY P.

"There's only one *X* that really matters right now," she said.

"Project PX!" said Akiko, dipping a cookie in her glass. "But what's left over when we spell that out? Josie, do you know anyone named Jack or Jacky?"

I shook my head and grabbed a pencil. We ticked off each of the letters that made up "Project PX."

What remained were three letters: A-K-Y.

"Kay!" we exclaimed in hushed shouts.

Now we had to figure out the last line. My heart beat like a drum corps, pounding so hard I thought Akiko and Mae had to be able to hear it. But when I listened to Akiko's noisy breathing and saw the flush in Mae's cheeks, I knew they were as anxious as I was. We stared:

HEN WOKS.

"My auntie woks," said Akiko quickly. "Lots of people I know cook with woks. But a hen?"

"Rearrange the letters," urged Mae, her usual serene calm forgotten now as the pressure mounted. Another news report drifted in from the radio, telling us of more losses for British and American troops, and I noticed the pencil in my hand begin to shake. We had to figure out Emmett's message! We had to stop the Hisser from committing another terrible attack! We had to do something—*right now!*—to beat this evil!

"Hew, how, new, now, snow, show, know," Akiko said, rearranging the letters of the third and final line.

"Know." Mae gasped in horror. "That's got to be it— using the *K*."

And at that moment, the whole puzzle seemed to click.

DANGER DANGER DANGER!
PROJECT PX KAY.
HE KNOWS.

Thirty-Three

"HE KNOWS!" MAE WHISPERED, TRYING HARD not to shriek. "Emmett is telling us the Hisser knows about Project PX! About Kay!"

We were on our feet in seconds, stumbling toward the kitchen window and onto the fire escape. I caught a glimpse of the clock on the wall as we left: It was ten minutes to midnight. Thankfully, Vinnie and Baby Lou didn't stir during our noisy escape to the roof.

"When we get to the Moore School," I began, barely able to find my voice as fear gripped my throat, "we need to move them safely out of the building. And at the same time, we cannot let Project PX—whatever it is—fall into the wrong hands."

It was my fault. I knew now that it had to be. But at the same time, this knowledge gave me a determination as strong as steel: I'd keep my cousin safe, and all of the Secret Six safe, even if it took every ounce of strength I had.

"And we need to finish off the Hisser and his henchmen, too," Akiko said. "Because if we don't stop them, they'll just come back stronger next time."

We stood close together, forming our familiar triangle, shoulders touching. The night was warm, and the moon shone bright on our faces as we looked into one another's eyes.

"Finish chewing already, Akiko!" said Mae, her voice impatient.

"It's been a tough day! And Lorna Doones are the best cookies ever made," Akiko said, her mouth full. Finally, she swallowed and dusted at the crumbs on her lips. "Okay. I'm ready."

All three of us seemed to know what to do now. Reaching into the center, we grabbed hold of one another's right hands. And just as we connected, the familiar surge of electricity pulsed through my veins. Mae's eyes were bright, and Akiko's raspy breathing was louder than ever.

"Cape," I whispered to the night.

"Mask," said Akiko.

"Boots," declared Mae.

Nothing happened. The quiet thrumming played in my ears, but where was the burst of light? The swirling air?

"We've lost it," said Akiko. "I knew it was too good to be true!"

"No, we haven't lost it," corrected Mae. "We're just not doing something right."

We clasped our hands tighter in the center of our triangle, and we each threw our left arms around the shoulders next to us.

"For Hauntima," said Mae.

"Right," added Akiko, sounding hopeful. "And Hopscotch."

"And for Zenobia, the Palomino," I urged, "Nova the Sunchaser, Miss Smash . . ."

The familiar yellow glow hummed around us, but our clothing was the same. What were we doing wrong?

"Maybe it's because you were still eating," said Mae, glaring at Akiko. "Do you still have cookies in one of your hands?"

"Or maybe you broke our powers," Akiko shot back, "and that's why I fell out of the sky earlier today."

Panicky tears filled my eyes, and I tilted my face to the stars, hoping to keep them from pouring down my cheeks. Kay was in danger! We had to act now to help save her!

"All I want is to protect the people I love from getting hurt," I shouted, no longer able to contain my frustration.

A beam of golden light shot from the center of our tri-angle, and a gust of wind lifted our hair. Mae and Akiko screamed in surprise.

"Right! Protect innocents and fight for justice," added Mae.

"And do good," hollered Akiko, though we could barely hear her as the crackling current began to pound in our ears and the swirling rush of wind and light whipped faster and faster into a funnel around us. It lifted us off our feet, and I had the sensation of being in the eye of a raging hurricane. Colors swam before me in bright green, bold purple, and radiant orange.

And then in a flash we catapulted back down onto the rooftop. In the stunned silence, we stared at one another. I was happy to have stayed on my feet this time, instead of landing on my backside like I'd done before. Mae wobbled in her boots, but she remained upright like me. Akiko stumbled and looked as if she were going to fall, but at the last moment she caught herself too. Maybe we were finally getting the hang of this.

"We're going to need names soon," said Akiko, running her gloved fingers across her orange mask. "Something better than 'Wee Three' or whatever the newspapers have called us."

"My aunt Willa back in Chicago has a pilot's license," said Mae, tugging at the top of her purple boot. "I've always wanted to wear boots like she wears when she flies. Maybe I should be called Super Boots!"

I ran my fingers over my own boots, tall and green. I touched the mask at my eyes too. The material seemed to pulsate under my fingers, as if it had an energy of its own.

"Look, you two, we don't have time to waste on names," I said, unfurling my emerald cape behind me as I leapt upward toward the full yellow moon. "If we don't stop this evil snake, our name won't matter. Nobody will remember it anyway."

Thirty-Four

*A*S ANYONE WITH A LITTLE FLYING EXPE-rience will say, soaring through the skies at night is a whole different thing from flying during the day. With the war on, the city was under a strict blackout order. And like most cities around the country, Philadelphia's stores, homes, and businesses weren't allowed to leave even a single light on. So Akiko, Mae, and I relied on the moon to help us get where we needed to be.

The redbrick buildings looked like dollhouses in a row as we soared high above the streets.

We were breathless by the time we landed at that famil-iar corner of Walnut and Thirty-Third Street. Unlike in the afternoon, when it had been bustling with college students and businesspeople coming and going, now it was deserted. Mae, Akiko, and I seemed to be the only souls, our moonlit shadows stretching into the empty intersection.

"Let's hide behind the newsstand and wait for them," said Akiko, pointing at the small building on the corner diagonal from Kay's building. "The moment they arrive, we'll knock them out cold."

"There's no sign the Hisser or his men are already here," said Mae, her eyes scanning the scene. "Just a few kids on their bikes over by that tree. One of them looks like that awful neighbor of yours, the bully."

This caught my attention. I stared toward the tree in the darkness. Wouldn't you know it, Toby and his band of juvenile delinquents were out past curfew. And riding my brothers' bikes.

"Come on," I said. "Let's go make sure justice is served."

Akiko, Mae, and I leapt into the air and circled above Toby and the other boys from our neighborhood. They were taunting a mother raccoon they'd snared with a rope, and her four young kits scampered around her in a sort of panic.

"Let that animal go," I called as we landed a few feet from Toby's circle. The boys jumped in surprise. "She's an innocent animal. Let her and her kits go right now."

"What have we here?" said Toby, pushing past his fellow lunkheads to get a better view of the three of us. "Some kiddies dressed up for a costume party. Halloween's not for three more months."

"Four," I corrected, "but math isn't for everyone."

"Hey, you better watch your mouth, girlie," he spat. "Or we'll use this rope on you trick-or-treaters."

Mae stepped forward now, and her voice was like ice. "You heard her. Set that animal free, or you will suffer the consequences."

Toby laughed at Mae, and his dim-witted buddies joined in.

"Right," he scoffed. "Like you're going to stop me." And to show he wasn't going to be pushed around, Toby yanked on the rope around the raccoon's neck, tightening it.

"Enough!" shouted Mae. And with a thrust of her hand, she unleashed a gale-force wind that knocked Toby and the other bullies to the ground.

As they climbed to their feet, Akiko transformed into a bowling ball and knocked Toby out at the knees. Again he fell to the ground, this time scraping the palms of his hands.

"Ouch!" he cried. "That really hurt!"

"Imagine how those animals feel when you torment them," I snapped. "But that's just it; you don't seem to understand how others feel. You only care about yourself."

Toby started to climb onto his bike seat as Mae freed the raccoon from the rope. The kits chased after their mama, racing for the nearest bushes. I was relieved to see the raccoons escape, but I couldn't bear to let Toby get away. So I scooped up all five of the bikes, including the red ones that belonged to Vinnie and Baby Lou, and held them above my head as I hovered in the air.

"I understand not all of these bikes are your own," I said in a voice low and steady. I didn't want to lash out in anger, the way I had at Gerda's Diner. I tried to be more like Zenobia and the Palomino and so many of the superheroes I admired—using power for justice, not vengeance. "Tomorrow morning, you will return what you've stolen to the rightful owners. If you don't, you'll hear from us again. And we won't be so nice."

And just to make sure I was getting through to these knuckleheads, I used a bit of telekinesis—staring at *one, two, three, four, five* heads, then flicking my eyes—to knock their skulls together. Toby stumbled backward, stared at me wild-eyed, and then took off running. His not-so-tough lunkheads followed close behind.

"What do you plan to do with those bikes?" asked Mae.

"I've got a good idea," I said, adjusting my hold on the bicycles. "After talking to Mr. Hunter last night about the stolen bikes, I thought it might make sense to park these in Toby's bedroom. Just to make sure he gets caught!"

Akiko was close beside me, and as one of the bikes started to slip, she grabbed hold of my arm. "If only we could teleport to Toby's apartment right now!"

With a *whoosh* filling my ears and a blinding light forcing me to squint, I began to slip downward as if I were on a long slide at the playground. Only, where I landed wasn't in a familiar park. It was in the bathtub of an unfamiliar bathroom.

"Josie!" whispered a sandpaper voice. "What did you just do?"

It was Akiko, still holding tight to the bicycle and to my arm.

"It wasn't me!" I gasped, my voice cracking. "You said it. I think you've got another superpower! Just like the Palomino: teleportation!"

"Only, where did it take us?" she croaked. "Let me try again!"

And she said something about teleporting to Toby's bedroom, not bathroom. With another *whoosh*, we seemed to slide through space again.

"This looks about right," I whispered, setting down the bikes beside a boyish-looking bed as quietly as I could. We leaned them together against a wall, beneath a photograph of Toby Hunter and his dad going fishing.

"Do you think he'll get in trouble?" Akiko asked.

"We can only hope," I whispered. "Now, let's get out of here. We can't leave Mae waiting!"

Akiko said something about wanting to teleport back to Mae, and with a noisy popping sound, she disappeared.

I was left standing alone in the awful silence of Toby Hunter's empty bedroom. Snores from the room next door droned through the wall. What if Mr. Hunter woke up and found me here?

I'd just contemplated climbing out the open window when another popping sound broke the silence.

"I think you have to hold on to make this work," Akiko whispered irritably, grabbing my hand. "Here we go!"

And in another flash of white light and a slide down what felt like a twisting chute, we landed right back on the street beside Mae.

"That was impressive," she said, clapping her purple-gloved hands. "Another power for you, Orange One. I hope that takes care of the bullies and stolen bikes. But now I think it's time we get back to protecting Kay and the computers. Come on!"

Mae was right. We couldn't afford to waste another moment where the Hisser was concerned. We raced back to the corner and stared at the Moore School's redbrick walls. The street was still quiet, and the full moon hung just above the treetops.

"We've got to work together to fight him," I whispered. "We know it's not just the Hisser who's after Project PX, but the Duke and his henchmen too. Whatever that secret project is, it's too important to let a bunch of Nazis make off with it!"

The silence was eerie as we crossed toward the school's

darkened front doors. The only sound was the faint whistle of a train in the distance. The blinds must have been drawn tight, because no light filtered out into the street.

"Oh, listen, here comes a dog and its owner," whispered Mae, spotting a pair moving slowly along the sidewalk not far from us. "Look at those droopy ears! I love basset hounds. This one's name is Bertha, and she is not happy about those men parked in the big station wagon with the wooden sides. One of them took her ball."

Akiko rolled her eyes and told Mae to can it.

"This isn't the right time for your dog obsession," she whispered sharply. "We've got to take this seriously."

"I am taking it seriously," Mae shot right back, her eyes studying the street up ahead where the basset hound was walking. "And so is Bertha!"

"Please," I snapped to halt their latest back-and-forth bickering. "Mae, we could use your telepathy to pick up what the Hisser or the Duke might be thinking around here. Not whether a dog lost his ball."

"*Her* ball," Mae corrected. "Bertha is a she."

Nevertheless, Mae stopped focusing on Bertha. Instead she pressed her hands to her temples and stepped out from the shadows, staring hard at the Moore School's two wooden doors and what lay inside. She seemed to focus her mind, so Akiko and I stepped to each side of her as watchers, wary of any movement in the darkness.

"Trying to find the Hisser . . . what he's thinking . . . ," Mae said slowly. Then, with a start, she grabbed us. "Oh no! The Hisser and his men are in that big wooden wagon Bertha saw! They're planning to attack . . .

"Now!"

A split second later, the street transformed from silence to a deafening roar.

"THE BRATS ARE BACK!" boomed the Hisser, his snakelike form bursting through a round sewer cover in the middle of the road before us. The metal disk clattered on the street like an oversize coin flung by a careless giant. And the force of his thunderous voice hurled us backward like rag dolls. Our bodies slammed into the wall of the brick building just behind us.

The Hisser's yellow snake eyes glared, and his scaly serpent's body seemed endless as it burst up and up and up from the dank underworld. The only difference in his appearance was on the right side of his gruesome head, which was red and blistery from a burn. Immediately I thought of Akiko and her power with flames.

"This is the end of the story for you, my tragic trinity," he hissed.

I pulled myself to my feet, rubbing the back of my head. I didn't think anything was broken, but my neck and back throbbed with pain.

"What's a trinity?" asked Akiko as Mae helped pull her

to her feet. "I've never heard that word before."

"You know," I said hurriedly, my eyes on the Hisser writhing before us. "Anything that comes in threes. Like if Hauntima, Hopscotch, and Nova the Sunchaser all fought bad guys together, as a team."

"Or Zenobia, the Palomino, and that wolfy sidekick the Palomino had, Star," Mae added.

"I forgot the Palomino had a dog," Akiko grunted in reply. "I like trinities."

Before we had time to say anything more, the Hisser flicked his dangerous rattlesnake tail and slammed it into the building just above our heads. Wood and bricks exploded into the air, then crashed down around us.

"Say your goodbyes, girlies." He laughed, his voice hitting us like a punch. Again we staggered backward from the force of it. "Because this battle is for grown-ups only!"

I picked up bricks in each hand as Akiko and Mae pulled themselves upright again. They came to stand on either side of me, holding bricks of their own. And while staring at the Hisser's slimy, slithering form made my knees want to buckle, I felt stronger knowing Mae and Akiko were beside me.

Hurling the bricks at the Hisser's dangerous, deadly form, I began to like the sound of "trinity" now too.

Thirty-Five

KIKO WAS AN ORANGE BLUR AS SHE SOARED
into the air and circled Kay's building, sizing up our battle
scene. "About twenty or so men," she called. "Maybe more."
Before long she joined Mae on the Moore School's rooftop.
Mae stood stock-still and again focused her powers on reading the Hisser's mind.

"He's thinking about breaking windows, maybe starting
a fire," Mae shouted as she read the oversize worm's evil
intentions. Akiko flung fireballs at his henchmen in the
street. I saw the Duke duck for cover behind what looked
a lot like an unmarked police wagon—long and brown with
wooden sides—barely escaping one of her flaming strikes.

And I caught sight of Harry Sawyer crawling behind the bumper of the Duke's curvy sedan across the street, his fedora smoking from a near miss.

Anger flared inside me at the thought of Harry's betrayal. While Akiko, Mae, and I were focused on Ursula, Harry had been one of the Duke's spies all along.

I turned away from Harry and spotted more men crouching low behind nearby cars, avoiding Akiko's fiery wrath and awaiting directions from their slimy boss, the Hisser himself. The number surprised me—the Hisser's nest of spies was bigger than I'd first imagined.

How could the three of us beat them?

There was no time to doubt myself. As we'd done with the Carson Building fire and the battle at the naval shipyard, we just had to step up and do the best we could. With Akiko and Mae busy on the rooftop, it was my turn to act—and fast. So I summoned all the strength I could muster, and I whispered into the night two of the most powerful words I could think of just then:

"I can."

Scrambling around for something to slow the Hisser down, I picked up a park bench that stood beside a lamppost. With all my might, I hurled it through the air at the hideous snake. "This is the end of you and your evil, Hisser!" I shouted. Then I saw a trash can, and I heaved that at him too. I passed two bicycles leaning near the bakery, and I flung them at his menacing shape.

They bumped against the Hisser's slimy scales and crashed to the ground.

"You're like a mosquito," he taunted, his laugh terrifying. "I hardly felt that!"

And as if to put me in my place, his deadly split tongue shot from his mouth and slammed me backward into the lamppost. My head rang like a telephone, but I had to shake it off. I stood up again and got my bearings.

"He's going to keep you busy in the street," shouted Mae from the rooftop, again reading the Hisser's thoughts, "so that the Duke and the other spies can slip inside!"

I dodged another swipe from the Hisser's forked tongue, making sure to avoid his dangerous hypnotic stare as well, and I took off toward Kay's door before the spies could get there. But movement to the right of me caught my attention. It was a group of what looked to be four college kids, laughing and talking as they passed down the street. At first they seemed oblivious to our battle, but then one of them caught sight of the Hisser's grotesque snake form, and he screamed.

"Too bad for you." The Hisser laughed, his venomous head bobbing and fangs glistening in the moonlight. "You're in the wrong place at just the right time!"

And he lunged at them.

I couldn't bear to watch innocent people get caught in

the Hisser's deadly game. So at the same moment that the Hisser lunged, I dove for the college students too.

With a sweep of my arms, I scooped up all four of them under their armpits and carried them halfway down the block. I dropped them safely in the grass, but as I let go, my left arm burned with pain.

"You're bleeding," called one of the students as I took to the sky again. "Hey, caped kid, are you all right?"

Flying back toward Kay's building, I touched my left shoulder and saw blood. One of the Hisser's razor-sharp fangs must have sliced my skin. Even if I had a way to bandage the wound, there was no time to fuss with it now. I'd have to remember to tell Mae and Akiko that our costumes didn't make us invincible.

They just made us think we were.

Back at the corner now, I hovered in the air and saw the Hisser make a go for the Moore School's front door. He bashed at it with his tail, bricks shattering into the air with every hit. The Duke, with his shiny monocle over one eye, stood laughing behind him, signaling for the rest of his spy conspirators to scurry into the building. Like a pack of rats, they emerged from their hiding spots and darted across the street.

I had to stop them from getting to Kay and the other computers. What would happen if they destroyed Project PX? Or stole it for the Nazis? And what would they do to my cousin and the other women if they caught them? Pressing on my bleeding shoulder and feeling the pain shoot through my arm, I didn't have to try hard to imagine how the Hisser would handle them.

"Knock, knock," the Hisser boomed, his earsplitting voice bursting the glass in the Moore School's windows. "Guess who's here."

Flying above the street, I looked around for a way to block his advance. With silent feet, I landed just behind him. Even though rage simmered inside me at the thought of Emmett kidnapped and Kay threatened, I tried not to act from anger. I wasn't after revenge. What I wanted more than anything was to protect Kay and Emmett—and the other puzzlers and computers.

And if I kept this secret project from falling into the wrong hands, maybe that would protect us all.

"Don't hesitate," came a voice hovering in the air beside me. "He may seem more powerful than you, but don't lose heart!"

It was Hauntima's ghost, fainter than ever but back again to guide us!

"I can smell victory," the Hisser boomed. "These caped crybabies are nothing more than gnats to me! But luckily, I come with a fly swatter!" And lifting his rattlesnake tail, he whipped it to the ground. The sidewalk crumbled under the force of it.

My throat went dry as a dustrag.

But Hauntima's silvery form was unfazed as she swept toward the curvy sedan parked near us. "Use your gifts and defeat this villain," she urged. "Hauntima wills it!"

The Hisser noticed Hauntima's ghost, and he issued a deafening laugh that burst the domed glass of the streetlights and made my head throb with pain.

"A ghostly superhero," he howled. "Where are the real ones? Like good old Hopscotch and the Stretcher and the rest? All tied up, I suspect?"

His scaly form was coiled in the middle of the street now, as his flat, deadly head bobbed back and forth, beady eyes studying Hauntima's vapory shape.

Now was my time to act. I wrapped my hands beneath the back bumper of the car. And with all my strength, I lifted it high into the air, balancing the silver-grilled front in both my hands.

"Look at her," shrieked one of the Duke's men to my left. "That green kid's lifting a car! Like Super—"

"Like the great Zenobia," hollered Mae, who swooped down from the rooftop and landed beside me.

"And Hauntima herself," added Akiko with a sneeze. *Ah-choo!* And suddenly the Duke's fedora crackled with sparks. "Not to mention Hopscotch and plenty of others."

"No, not Hopscotch," corrected Mae. "She doesn't have superpowers. She's just got great fighting skills along with that mask that keeps her secret. You mean Nova the Sunchaser."

"Oh, you're right," Akiko said with annoyance. "Again."

"And there's Miss Smash and the Rebelle in Red," continued Mae. "They have great costumes but not super-strength like the others."

"Okay already," snapped Akiko. "You're right. You're right! It's kind of getting annoying!"

"I am not trying to be annoying," Mae told Akiko. "I am trying to be accurate."

I didn't have time to jump into their latest argument. With the shiny car balanced above my head, I tottered closer toward the Hisser. And using all the strength I could muster—and with searing pain shooting through my left shoulder—I heaved the car forward. It landed on the Hisser's deadly tail with a devastating thud.

"Should we save Harry while the Hisser's distracted?" called Akiko in a hushed voice. "I can transform into a net and snatch him to safety."

"Or I can try to make it snow on him," offered Mae, "maybe make him too cold to join with the bad guys."

I could barely choke out the words. "Leave him."

Akiko and Mae shook their heads like they didn't understand.

"Just trust me on this one, okay?" I said, trying to be heard despite the Hisser's furious shrieking. It shattered the windows of every car around us.

"Trust you?" echoed Mae, and her gaze was steady and knowing.

"What do you mean?" pressed Akiko. "We thought Harry Sawyer was your friend. I'm confused."

"He acted like my friend," I said, my heart squeezing at the thought of his betrayal. "It's so hard to admit how wrong I was. But I have to tell you:

"Harry is one of them, one of the bad guys."

Akiko looked stunned. Mae seemed sad.

"I should have told you sooner," I said, desperate to get into the building and save Kay. "But it's not easy to admit to you both that I'd been such a fool. Sometimes telling the truth, knowing I'm going to let somebody down . . . It's too hard.

"I'm sorry."

"What about Ursula?" whispered Akiko. "I thought she was the spy. . . ."

Mae reached over and clasped my hand. "It's okay," she whispered. "You're not a fool. You're a friend, and you trusted someone."

Akiko punched me in my good arm. "We'll stop Harry and all of these dopes. Now, let's quit gabbing and go!"

Mae jumped into action, raising her arms and summoning the wind. Lightning crackled in the sky, and rain began to pour down in sheets. She was kicking up a hurricane!

"You've got to get inside," Mae called to us. "I'll keep

them back for as long as I can. It's up to you both to warn the computers!"

Akiko and I raced for the Moore School's entrance. She grabbed the knob and rattled the wooden door with all her might.

"It's locked," she shouted, her voice barely audible over Mae's howling storm and the Hisser's angry wailing. "What do we do now?"

"We're superheroes, remember?" I said, wanting to laugh despite the danger. "We can't be stopped by a little locked door!"

I stared at the doorknob, squinting and trying hard to use the power of my mind to flip the dead bolt. But before I managed to make the lock turn, my concentration was interrupted by Akiko's sudden sneezing. Flames shot from her mouth and nose, the way I imagined a dragon might breathe fire. And suddenly the wooden door was engulfed in fire.

Black embers fluttered to the floor at our feet, and with one nudge from Akiko's shoulder, the entire door caved in. We slipped through the charred opening and heaved a sigh of relief.

"I could get used to this." She laughed.

Me too.

"Now let's find my cousin and the other computers," I said, racing toward the staircase. "And Project PX!"

Thirty - Seven

I STAGGERED BACKWARD, MY MIND REELING so fast it made me lose my balance. Harry was a double agent? Not someone who had betrayed my trust? I wanted to throw my arms around him in a big hug, but I couldn't let myself. Harry had no idea who the three caped heroes standing before him were, and I wasn't about to give myself away. If I knew anything about anything, it was that superheroes never revealed their true identities.

Akiko and Mae stood there slack-jawed and staring at Harry too, so I could tell they were just as stunned. And while this was all only a momentary distraction, it was enough time for the Hisser to act.

"Traitorous scum!" he hissed, breaking free of the FBI agents' handcuffs as he transformed again. "You may have deceived me, but you'll never stop me!"

The Hisser's hideous snake form filled the room, his scaly, serpentine body slithering around and around in a dizzying, hypnotic threat. With a whip of his rattlesnake tail, he swatted Harry and the agents. They flew backward, slamming into the blinking black steel of the ENIAC machine.

"These computers are mine now," he announced, yellow eyes blazing and fangs flashing as his deadly coils wrapped around Kay, Jean, and the rest of the ENIAC Six. In one fluid motion, his slimy body squeezed, trapping them in his hideous grip. And he slithered toward the door. Before I could leap after them, he was gone.

"No," I shouted, looking for something to throw at his retreating form. "Leave them alone!"

Hauntima's pale shape hovered overhead as we chased the Hisser into the night. "Don't give up," she urged, though her ghostly outline was quickly disappearing now. "Though evil may seem to be winning, it shall never triumph. So long as there are good people willing to fight!"

"Don't go," Akiko called, her voice pained. "We need you, Hauntima! We're not ready!"

"It is we who need you," Hauntima said, her silvery form almost transparent. She was like a bubble floating in the moonlight. I reached out my hand as if to touch her. "The three of you—you're our last hope."

And then she was gone. Akiko, Mae, and I were on our own.

"Let's keep after him," I shouted. And concentrating on my telekinesis, I began to fling whatever I could at the Hisser's scaly head—potted plants, rocks, even another trash can. Mae bounded behind me, hurling lightning bolts like javelins, while Akiko shape-shifted into animal form.

"An otter? What are you thinking?" hollered Mae as she caught sight of Akiko's furry new body. "Otters aren't scary! What do you plan to do, kill him with cuteness?"

"I'm a mongoose, not an otter!" answered Akiko testily. "The mongoose is a snake's worst enemy!" And she lunged for the Hisser's throat with her sharp front teeth as Mae and I dodged out of the way.

I soared high above them to get a better view. And that's when I noticed the big wooden station wagon parked across the street again. I'd seen it before, when we'd first begun fighting off the Hisser and his bullies, but I hadn't paid much attention to it. Now the wagon's back doors were open, and I could see a few figures sitting on benches inside.

"Help!" one of them shouted. "Get us out of here!"

I recognized that voice right away. It was Emmett!

I swooped down to the wagon doors and hovered in the air as I peered inside. Emmett's arms and legs were bound in rope, but he'd been able to slip off the gag that was wrapped around his mouth and shout for help. Four other boys were with him, tied up the same way. They must have been the other puzzlers!

"Be gone with you, Emerald Irritant!" bellowed the Hisser. And his booming voice hit me like a fist, sending me crashing backward through the window of the nearby bakery. Shards of glass shattered into the air. "These puzzlers are mine!"

Kay and Jean, along with Marlyn, Ruth, Betty, and Fran, pounded on the Hisser's scaly skin. But he would not release his grip, shoving them into the wagon with the others before transforming back to his human shape. "And now that I have the computers, too, our army will be unstoppable," he said, slamming the back door on the wood-paneled wagon. "Farewell, losers! My submarine awaits!"

Snatching the sharp-edged fedora off his head, he whipped it at Mae and Akiko, who had come to rest on the sidewalk near the park. They ducked just in time, as his dangerous hat sliced through the air, the razor-sharp rim piercing the moonlight. Branches from the trees just overhead fell to the ground in its wake, cut down by the hat's deadly brim.

Diving behind the steering wheel, the Hisser took off down the street, tires squealing as he made his escape.

"We can't let him get to his submarine," I called to

Akiko and Mae. "He's got Kay in that wagon! And Emmett too! We have to save them—and all the others."

The three of us took to the sky and raced right behind him, the wagon's headlights making the Hisser easy to spot on the dark boulevards below. Without even having to utter a word, we seemed to know just what to do. Using our separate powers that made us each so special, we would find a way to defeat the Hisser—together.

Akiko sprinted ahead of us, shape-shifting into what must have been a cheetah, judging by her speed. Racing alongside the Hisser, she distracted his driving, causing the wagon to career wildly down the nearly empty road.

"He's going to turn left up ahead and drive along the park pathway," Mae shouted, using her telepathy power. "He thinks he can get rid of Akiko that way!"

"Don't say our names out loud," I reminded her. "We can't let our real identities slip out!"

"Then we'd better come up with some names, Greenie! Now do your thing before he gets away!"

The wagon pulled to the left, just as Mae said it would. Only, the Hisser's route turned crazy as he popped the vehicle over curbs and scraped into a few park benches. Then, still trying to shake off Akiko, he sped up even more and raced past a pond toward the center of the park, where a low fountain was spraying water.

I stared up ahead at the stone statue that stood in the

middle of the fountain. It looked familiar—a marble warrior, one arm raised in battle. Using all my powers of concentration, I imagined the statue ripping off its pedestal and hurtling into the path of the Hisser's oncoming car.

As soon as I thought it, the statue followed the direction of my eyes and soared through the air, landing just in front of the Hisser's wagon. Brakes screeched, but there was no time for the Hisser to stop. The wagon's front end crumpled like an accordion.

"Well done," cheered Mae. "He's stuck now!"

The wagon's horn blared into the night. With Akiko back in her superhero form now, the three of us rushed to the scene and opened the driver's door, ready for more battle.

But the Hisser was still stunned from the crash, and before he could act, Mae slammed the door shut. Suddenly rain began to pour inside the wagon, over the Hisser's head.

"Snakes hate rain." She smiled. "This should keep him miserable and powerless long enough for the cops to arrive."

With Mae covering the Hisser, Akiko and I raced to the back and flung open the wagon's rear doors. We snapped Emmett's ropes as Kay, Jean, and all of the computers and puzzlers climbed out.

"You guys are amazing," said Emmett, catching his breath as police sirens grew closer. "Who are you?"

I shrugged, barely able to keep myself from throwing

my arms around Emmett's neck and giving him a big hug. He was safe, finally!

"Who are we?" I asked, hoping my voice didn't give away my identity. "We're still working on that."

Emmett nodded excitedly, running his hand over his wrist where the rope had been tied. "I wish my friend Josie were here to see this! She doesn't shut up about superheroes! Josie's never going to believe me when I tell her that some kids saved us.

"And not just any kids. *Girls!*"

Thirty-Eight

$\mathcal{T}$HE POLICE ARE HEADING OVER," WHISPERED Mae a short time later. "I think we'd better get out of here. We don't want to have to answer too many questions."

"Plus," added Akiko, "I think I see your mom and brothers over there, getting out of that police car."

The night was lit up with the red lights of police cruisers, fire trucks, ambulances, and what must have been FBI cars. As we leapt into the night sky and circled over the leafy park, a cheer erupted below us.

Baby Lou's voice rose above the murmur of the crowd. "Look at those thupers! Vinnie told me he watched them earlier tonight, flying right over our apartment building!"

Vinnie was pointing up at us, beside Lou. "The radio report called that bright one the Orange Inferno," he shouted, always ready with the facts, even when he's half asleep and wearing his pajamas. "And the other one was called the Violet Vortex—I think the reporter said he'd seen her stir up a hurricane and everything!"

We circled through the treetops until we found an isolated place to land around the far side of the pond. Once we were on the ground, we transformed back into our regular selves and tried to catch our breath.

"Did you hear Josie's little brothers?" asked Akiko with a gravelly laugh. "The Orange Inferno. I like the sound of that!"

"It's not bad," said Mae, smoothing down her hair and keeping pace with Akiko as we headed right back toward the growing crowd at the fountain. "But let's face it, the Violet Vortex is pretty inspired. It sounds kind of dainty, like a flower, while at the same time intimidating."

"What name did they give you, Josie?" asked Akiko. "I didn't hear Vinnie say anything about you."

I was walking in between them, but my steps were faster. I hadn't heard Vinnie mention me either. But it didn't matter, because I'd already made up my mind.

"You could be the Green Guard," suggested Mae, giving me an encouraging look. "What do you think of that? Though maybe that sounds more like a big shrub for a garden rather than a superhero."

"What about the Mighty Gardener?" said Akiko. "You know, you're green like a garden, and you've got the super-strength. . . . It's fitting. Or maybe the Mossy Boss? Or—"

"Or maybe we should focus on Emmett and Kay and the ENIAC machine and what's left of the basement," I suggested, unable to hide the edge in my voice. We'd just battled one of the worst supervillains to hit town in years, and all they cared about was playing a name game? We needed to make sure the cops took the Hisser away and check on Kay, not to mention sort things out with Mrs. B.

"Anyway," I said, stiffening my spine and throwing my shoulders back the way I'd seen Mrs. B do earlier today, "I think I should name myself. Why let some strangers do it? If true power comes from inside us, like Hauntima said, then that's where my name is going to come from: me."

We rounded the corner and headed for the cluster of familiar faces. Emmett and the puzzlers were talking with the police. My family had moved away from the Hisser's wagon and was standing off to the side, far from the rest of the crowd. Mam was looking worried as she pulled Vinnie and Baby Lou closer.

"Josie, where have you been?" she called, relief washing over her as we raced to her side. "There's been a terrible incident with Kay and the people she works with. I'd just gotten home when the police called. They sent a car around to get us. The boys were asleep, but you were gone. . . ."

I'd forgotten about that little detail—how to explain why I'd left my brothers alone in the apartment. I moved my mouth to speak, but no sound came out.

"Please don't be mad at Josie," said a voice. "She's a good kid."

I looked up and saw Harry Sawyer—make that Bill Sebold—standing there. His face looked exhausted, but his eyes glowed with a sort of hopeful glimmer.

"She works hard at the diner for Gerda Gutler and me," he said. "And when Josie isn't busy with the tables and the dishes, she's helping me with the accounting. She's very smart, your daughter. She tells me all the time about her dream to study math like her cousin. What's her name? Cousin Kay?"

And just then Kay and the other women computers emerged from the police huddle. Mam stepped over and clasped Kay's hands, clearly overwhelmed with relief. Vinnie raced to her side, throwing his arms around her hips and practically knocking her over with his boisterous affection. Baby Lou ran too, though the green blanket wrapped around his shoulders made it hard for him to keep his balance.

"Josie," came Emmett's voice as he joined Harry, Mae, Akiko, and me, "you should have seen who was here earlier. Superheroes! Real ones!"

I smiled awkwardly and pretended disappointment that I'd missed them. But with the boys busy hugging Kay,

Harry wanted a moment to talk. He turned to me, his expression somber.

"Josie, I spoke a little bit with your brothers. They told me all about your dad," he said. I had to remind myself he was Bill now, not Harry. "To have fought so bravely at Pearl Harbor and the other battles, saving his men. I wish him well. Truly, your father is a hero."

I wanted to break away, to race over to Kay's side like my brothers and get lost in a hug. But I couldn't make my feet move.

"Not *is*," I said softly. "*Was*. My father *was* a hero."

My eyes stung, and I could feel Mae, Akiko, and Emmett staring at me.

"Dad was killed about ten days ago on an island in the Pacific. Mam got the telegram on Monday."

My throat was so tight, I could barely get the words out. Emmett put his arm around my shoulder. Akiko and Mae held my hands.

"The truth of it hurts so much—that someone we love more than anything is gone. Forever. We wanted to tell Vinnie and Lou, but Mam couldn't do it. And neither could I. So I kept Dad alive in our bedtime stories. He's like a caped hero now, someone from our comic books."

I shifted self-consciously as Kay and my family approached. We all have our ways of protecting our families.

This was mine.

"But we'll have to tell them about Dad tonight, before Toby Hunter does it. Toby saw the telegram delivered that day," I said, wiping at a tear. "When the priest comes round with the Western Union deliveryman, it's never good news. Everybody knows that. So now Toby's in on my secret, and he wants to hurt me with it."

I thought about those stolen bikes we'd left in his room. When Toby's dad found them tomorrow, he was going to explode. And Toby would be in big trouble. Which meant he'd come looking for revenge. He wouldn't care how much it'd hurt Vinnie and Lou to hear about Dad.

I couldn't go on. The words got knotted up in my throat. Emmett squeezed my shoulder, and Bill bowed his head. We stood together in the silence, and for the first time in a long while, a weight lifted from my chest. Mam and I were going to have to be honest with Vinnie and Lou, and it was going to hurt. But at least Toby Hunter wouldn't have power over me anymore.

When Kay finally stepped over to our circle, I flung my arms around her. And even though my body ached from battling with the Hisser, it was the sight of my cousin safe and sound that brought the flood of tears.

"I'm okay, Josie. Please don't worry. I can hardly believe tonight," Kay said a little breathlessly. "You'll read about it in the papers tomorrow. But let me say that I am fine and so are my colleagues. We were ready to do what was necessary to protect ourselves and our project. But the amazing part—we were assisted by the most remarkable superheroes. You would have loved it!"

I reached over to Baby Lou and tugged on the green blanket he'd wrapped himself in. There was enough of it to throw over Kay's shoulders and Vinnie's, too, on the other side of her. And even Mam, pressed in on the far end. They stepped closer into the circle with Akiko, Mae, Emmett, and me, and Bill, too, holding tightly to one another.

And to my blanket.

"That reminds me of your cape," whispered Mae, pointing. "As if—"

"As if it's protecting your family," interrupted Akiko.

And that's exactly how I saw it too. No matter what was ahead for us—battling Nazis and supervillains, defending top secret projects like the electronic computer, even saving innocent lives from evil—it all came down to these people. I would do anything to protect the people I loved. And I knew Mae and Akiko felt the same way.

"Were they brave, Kay, these superheroes?" asked Akiko, eager to hear more. "Brave and bold? Courageous and strong?"

"Yes, of course," Kay agreed. "One had amazing powers to create wind and rain—"

"Atmokinesis," announced Vinnie. "Just like Zenobia."

"Right, and another had the ability to produce fire and flames, which was stunning—"

"Pyrokinesis," interrupted Akiko with a nod to Vinnie, "like Hauntima." They both seemed to live for the times when they could show off their knowledge of random facts. I didn't know which of them was more annoying. And endearing. "That's the name for it, or so I've read in comic books."

Vinnie nodded his approval.

"There were some truly terrible goons in the room," Kay said, "real meanies, as Lou would say." And then, for the first time, she seemed to notice Harry Sawyer standing in our circle, and she flinched. "You! I thought you were one of them. But the FBI says you're on our side. Harry or William—what was your name? They said you were a double agent."

"Double agent?" exclaimed my mom, nearly jumping out of her shoes. "FBI? Kay, what else happened tonight?"

Thirty-Nine

I THINK I'VE MET YOU BEFORE, THROUGH Josie," Kay continued, as if not even hearing Mam. "You're her friend from the diner. Isn't that right, Josie?"

"Josie knew me as Harry Sawyer," he said, looking a little embarrassed, "but as you heard the agent say earlier, my real name is William Sebold. Please, call me Bill."

I smiled at Harry—*Bill*—and acted as surprised as Mam. But really what I felt was relief. When I thought he had been dishonest all this time, the betrayal hurt like a bee-sting. But now that I knew the story behind it, I could understand.

"Yes, Josie has been a good friend to me," Bill went on.

"When so many people had harsh words for Germans, Josie showed me kindness. She saw me as a human being first and not as a foreigner to be feared."

I shrugged, embarrassed by the attention.

"Sure there are Germans who are Nazis," I explained, talking more to my feet than to their faces. "But there are plenty who are just like you and me—good people who love their families and want to, you know, live their lives."

"But only a few who are double agents," said Akiko, smiling at Bill.

Suddenly I noticed a flashbulb pop behind Mam as a newspaper photographer snapped our picture. Two more joined him, and a handful of reporters, too. Their notepads were out as they fired off questions toward Kay and Bill and the rest of the women computers—the ENIAC Six—gathered in their own circle just beside us.

They were even taking pictures of the wrecked wagon.

"The statue doesn't seem to be damaged," said one of the photographers. "But I wonder what it will cost to move it back onto its pedestal."

"Kind of fitting, don't you think?" asked a reporter. "That this Zenobia statue is what finally brought the Hisser's fiendish career to a crashing halt? If I recall right, he's the one who nearly destroyed her sister's leg in one of their battles."

My jaw dropped, and Akiko and Mae looked just as stunned. That's when it hit me where we were: at the same park as yesterday when we took Mae's oath of secrecy. We stood on our tiptoes to get a better look at the white marble superhero that was now resting before the crumpled metal hood. Across the base was etched a single name:

ZENOBIA

I couldn't stop the smile that broke out across my face. I glanced at Mae and Akiko, who had plenty of questions for my cousin.

"What was the other caped hero like?" Mae asked eagerly.

"You talked about two of them," added Akiko. "What about the third one?"

Kay's face lit up. "Right-e-o! The third one wore a cape of the deepest green. She seemed to have superstrength, and she used it to protect the six of us from harm."

"And the power to move things with her mind," interjected Bill. "What is that called?"

At the same time, Akiko, Vinnie, and now Mae answered: "Telekinesis."

"That's right," Bill agreed. "She used it smartly, not in a violent manner. More, as Kay says, to protect than to lash out."

The reporters began to holler to one another, and more cameras lit up the night. "Did you hear that, fellas?" shouted one of them off to the left of me. "The Green Do-Gooder! She protects while she pummels!"

"That's not her name," shouted another reporter. "The Emerald Equalizer sounds more like it. She crushes the enemy with her superstrength."

"You're wrong," I said, turning to the reporters, my heart banging in my chest. I didn't want to give anything away about Akiko, Mae, and me, but I just had to set things straight. "I know about the green one.

"She's called the Emerald Shield. She wants to do good in the world—fight for justice and fairness and protect the innocent, just like her friends the Violet Vortex and the Orange Inferno. They might look different, but they're a trio, you know. Three apart, one together."

"Triple thuperheroes," said Baby Lou, leaping out from under the blanket. "With a million, jillion, infinity powers."

Vinnie joined him as they pretended to soar into the air. "They're three of a kind—a trinity. With powers to infinity!"

Forty

$\mathcal{T}$HE HEADLINES AT BREAKFAST WERE IMPOS-
sible to miss:

INFINITY TRINITY SAVES CITY

FBI WRAPS UP SPY CASE WITH HELP OF
INFINITY TRINITY

NAZI PLOT UNDONE BY INFINITY TRINITY

Too excited to sleep late, we were sitting in a booth at
Gerda's Diner and devouring our usual milkshakes and

pie, even though it was so early that the breakfast crowd hadn't even arrived. We ate up the news, too.

"This story says the doors and windows will be replaced at the Moore School today," said Akiko, pointing with her milkshake spoon at an article on the front page of the *Inquirer*. "Sounds like Kay and the other ENIAC Six will hardly have to miss a day of work."

"Which means the Duke and his spies didn't stop Project PX," I said, pausing to take a slurp of my brown cow. "And the Nazis won't get their hands on the electronic computer after all."

Mae rolled her eyes and dabbed her napkin to her lips. "Okay, okay, you can talk all morning about the FBI and breaking up the Duke's spy ring and saving the entire metropolitan Philadelphia area," she said in that patient way of hers. "But seriously, are neither of you going to say anything about this?"

She held up the front of the *Record*. Splashed across the top half of the page was a photograph of the three of us battling the Hisser. It was probably taken over the naval shipyard yesterday afternoon, which felt like a hundred years ago.

"Check out our form," croaked Akiko. "We're as dangerous as any squadron of bombers over Europe. I just wish these pictures were in color, so everyone could see my orange cape!"

"You are pretty good fliers," came a voice, "for novices.

But you'll have to work on some of the other powers. Especially when sneezing."

Akiko began to choke on her egg cream. Mae and I turned our heads to see who was speaking.

It was Mrs. B! She looked sharp in a red linen jacket and a red pillbox hat with a net veil draped over the top part of her face. Her expression was deadly serious, but her eyes held a certain twinkle that gave me the impression she was teasing us.

"May I join you?" she asked after a few moments of our stunned silence. "We have a great deal to discuss."

Since Akiko and I were seated together on one side of the table, Mae quickly slid closer to the window and made room. Mrs. B draped her jacket over an empty chair at the table beside us, then pushed the netting up on her hat. With an awkward limp from her bad leg, she slid into the booth. And after glancing at the newspaper headlines for a moment or two, she stacked the papers in a tidy pile and folded her hands on top of them.

"Where to begin?" she said, looking hard into first Mae's face, then Akiko's, and then into mine. "A lot has happened to you in a short time. I commend your work last night protecting Project PX and overpowering the spy ring. As you can imagine, we feel there's no turning back now."

My fork dropped with a noisy clatter. I pushed my plate away and wrapped my hands around the base of my milkshake, trying to settle my nerves.

"I guess you could, of course, choose not to join our league of secret heroes," she continued, ignoring my clumsiness. "But from what I have seen of the three of you together, and from what I observed before you stepped through our door a few days ago, each of you feels a very personal calling to fight injustice.

"I am grateful that you answered that call so passionately. Your efforts to stop the notorious international villain Hank Hissler, also known by his more infamous title, the Hisser, were superb. We at Room Twelve thank you."

My jaw hung open in surprise, and I felt a swift kick under the table from Mae, who gestured for me to close it. She gave a little *ahem* and sat up straighter in her seat, while Akiko pushed ahead with questions.

"What happened to all the bad guys he was working with?" she asked. "Have they been found? And will they go to prison? Because they're not anybody I'd like to run into again, even if I'm wearing a cape, a mask, and boots."

Mrs. B gave an encouraging nod. "First, Hank Hissler has already arrived at a high-security prison, where he will spend the rest of his life locked away in a cold, dark cell. They know how to keep reptiles in line. So you may rest assured that you will not encounter him or any of his dastardly henchmen—the Duke and the other spies—ever again."

Akiko let out a sigh of relief, and Mae wiped her brow. It was comforting to know the Hisser was no more.

"And what about Emmett and the puzzlers?" I asked. "What about all the people the Hisser grabbed to do the Nazis' dirty work?"

Mrs. B sat perfectly still. It was as if a cloud passed behind her eyes. Sadness had a way of doing that to people. I saw it with Mam's eyes now, especially when things reminded her of my dad—when we saw families out together or little kids riding on their fathers' shoulders. I could tell Mrs. B was missing someone.

"The puzzlers whom you girls know about—the children such as your friend Emmett Shea and the other kidnapped boys," she began. "They have been interviewed by Room Twelve and returned to their homes, safe and sound. The remarkable women known as the ENIAC Six as well."

And now she sighed, pausing just long enough for Gerda to fill her coffee cup and say a few pleasantries. Once Gerda was out of earshot, she went on.

"There have been others taken by villains. Many others," Mrs. B said. Her eyes were pained as she looked at the three of us. "And this is where you come in."

"What does all this have to do with us?" asked Akiko. "Why do you want some goofy kids like us on your side?"

"Not goofy," corrected Mae. "More like well-meaning."

"You're plenty goofy," argued Akiko, "the way you're always talking to animals like they're human beings and going on about those books you've read at your granny's library."

"That's called being compassionate. And smart," Mae argued back, her voice quiet but sharp. "It's not goofy."

I kicked them both under the table.

"As you've seen with Josie's cousin Kay McNulty and the rest of the ENIAC Six," Mrs. B explained, "not all superheroes wear capes. And their superpowers might not be so easy to detect at first. But what they do is nonetheless extraordinary."

I couldn't help but smile at the thought of Kay, Jean, Marlyn, Ruth, Betty, and Fran. Their math minds were their superpowers. The realization left me a little stunned:

Superheroes exist all around us, every day. Only, their costuming might not look so obvious.

"Hauntima," I began, still puzzling over how she fit in. "How did she know to help us?"

"And why was it only her ghost," added Mae, "and not the real superhero?"

Mrs. B lowered her hands to her lap, and her expression was serious—almost dark. Akiko, Mae, and I shot looks back and forth in the heavy silence.

"This is the task at hand," she said, her quick eyes meeting ours again. I sat up straighter, on the edge of my seat now. "Let me make it clear that Room Twelve believes you possess great promise in our fight for good. So if you feel up to the challenge, I'd like to ask you to join us on our next mission."

"Of course!" shouted Akiko, drawing a few stares from the other tables. Then whispering, "Are you kidding?"

"She means yes," Mae offered politely. "We'd be honored, ma'am."

"Where and when? We need details, what's expected of us," I began, making a list in my head of what we would have to do to get prepared. "Should we come with you now? Tell our families we'll be gone? Do we pack a suitcase?"

Mrs. B patted my hand, radiating a sense of calm.

"When the world needs a hero, that's what we become. It's as easy as that, no?" she said, getting to her feet with a little wince. Her leg must have been bothering her. "It's not until we're tested that we realize what powers we possess."

Mrs. B stood at the edge of our table and unfolded the newspapers, lining up the front pages next to each other. "In the meantime, enjoy the news accounts of the Orange Inferno, the Violet Vortex, and the Emerald Shield. It's been many years since Zenobia and the Palomino watched over the innocent. With your Infinity Trinity, the newspapers appear to be thrilled to once again have heroes to write about."

All three of us piped up with more questions, but Mrs. B just collected her things.

"Room Twelve has uncovered plots—in San Francisco, Chicago, Texas, even France—that might require extra attention," she said, slipping the netting lower on her hat so it concealed her eyes. "I will be in touch again, most likely quite soon."

With a slight bow she turned and walked away.

I stared after her, watching as she draped the red linen jacket over her shoulders. The way it hung to the floor as she passed Gerda and Bill at the counter—nearly touching the ankles of her trim black boots—reminded me of a cape. And that hat with the stylish flourish, the veil down so it covered her eyes. It was almost like a mask.

Mask?

My eyes darted to her feet again. *Boots?*

And that jacket! *Cape?*

And suddenly it hit me. I turned back toward the table and clutched my glass. So much of what had happened over the past few days had tumbled by in a blur. But now time slowed down. I could almost hear the thoughts in my mind finally clicking together like puzzle pieces.

"Hold on," I said, practically climbing over the booth seat as I pointed out the window. Mrs. B was there on the sidewalk, untying Astra's leash from a light pole. Mae and Akiko watched her too. "How did Mrs. B know to warn us about the Hisser's gaze? She said it could mesmerize. That he'd strike the moment those horrible yellow eyes flashed to red. And she was right!"

Akiko's breathing became louder.

"Think about it," she said, trying to whisper. "The only way you'd know something like that—"

"—is if you battled the Hisser yourself," said Mae, interrupting Akiko for the first time.

"And she's got that limp," I added. "Can you think of a superhero who had a devastating injury . . . ?"

"The Palomino did!" croaked Akiko. "It nearly killed her."

"And the Palomino had a sidekick!" said Mae, gazing out the window again at the retreating figures of Mrs. B and Astra. "A brilliant dog named Star."

My skin began to tingle from the crown of my head all the way to my feet. Mae's jaw dropped open so wide, she could have caught a pigeon. And Akiko began a coughing fit that prompted us to pass her our water glasses.

"Hauntima's ghost!" she sputtered in her gravelly whisper. "Is it really possible that Mrs. B could be the Palomino? And Astra could be Star?"

We turned from the window and scooted together in the booth, leaning in close to unravel the past days' mysteries. I stared at my blueberry pie, my head dizzy. Mrs. B's words echoed in my mind.

There have been others taken by villains. Many others.

And this is where you come in.

"That's it," I whispered, finally connecting the dots. The superheroes hadn't quit. They'd been kidnapped! I imagined Mrs. B's bright eyes and that cloud of sadness that sometimes passed behind them. "She's definitely the Palomino. Which means her sister is—"

"Zenobia!" interrupted Akiko.

"Zenobia, the greatest superhero of all time," agreed Mae, her voice reverent.

"Zenobia," I said, grabbing each of their hands. "And it's up to us to save her."

AUTHOR'S NOTE

$\mathcal{S}$TORIES ARE OFTEN WRITTEN TO ANSWER A question. In the case of *Cape*, I was asking a simple one: *Who came before Wonder Woman?* She arrived in December 1941. Was she the first superheroine? I wondered whether there had been others.

There had. Fantomah, who made her debut in *Jungle Comics* No. 2 in February 1940, nearly two years before Wonder Woman, is considered the first female comic book superhero. My character Hauntima is meant to honor Fantomah's strange, skull-faced powers.

And as I researched about other early superheroines, I was equally thrilled to read the accounts of real-life women heroes of the war: the original computer programmers, brilliant code crackers, daring airplane pilots, and even danger-loving spies, all of whom were doing groundbreaking, breathtaking things too.

In weaving these stories together, I wanted to spark the idea that superheroes are all around us—they just might not be wearing capes.

The Golden Age of Comic Books spanned the World War II years. And as women joined the workforce in record numbers—six and a half million filling jobs in factories and even the military—they became a bigger presence in comic books too. At its peak, Wonder Woman's comic book sold a staggering two and a half million copies each month, according to Trina Robbins in *The Great Women Superheroes*. With Cape, I tried to merge the spirit of powerful female comic book figures with the real-life women of the same era who stepped forward to do their part to fight evil and injustice in the world.

What follows is an explanation of some of the facts and historical figures who inspired the fiction in *Cape*. I hope you'll take a moment to explore more about these remarkable women and men and their bold, adventurous, even *super* feats. Visit my website, KateHannigan.com, for a curriculum guide and source material, and the history of Fantomah and other early comic book heroines who inspired the ones in my book.

The ENIAC Six

Who were the ENIAC Six? As Jean Jennings Bartik wrote in her autobiography, *Pioneer Programmer: Jean Jennings Bartik and the Computer that Changed the World*, they were "six women who had the guts to pursue their dreams and in doing so made a small, but important mark in the pages of history."

The Electronic Numerical Integrator and Computer, or ENIAC, marked the start of the modern computer age. When I first heard about the ENIAC, I was intrigued, both as a milestone for human development but also on a more personal level: because my grandfather Bill Nolan was one of many workers who helped construct it by moonlighting for the Moore School of Electrical Engineering at the University of Pennsylvania. The ENIAC was so top secret, he didn't talk to his family about the work, and he didn't even know what function the machine would have—only that it was meant to help in the war effort.

As I read more about the key players involved with the ENIAC, I became fascinated by the ENIAC Six and one woman in particular: Kathleen "Kay" McNulty. Like my grandparents on my father's side, Kay was born in County Donegal, Ireland, into a household of Irish or "Gaelic" speakers—meaning they did not speak English at home. Kay's father immigrated to Philadelphia in 1923, the year my grandparents left County Donegal and did the same.

I found it intriguing that Kay, an immigrant who spoke

no English when she arrived, went on to contribute so tremendously to one of America's greatest accomplishments: the first electronic computer, the one to which all other computers today can trace their DNA. Kay's story of hard work and success echoes those of millions of other immigrants.

Kay McNulty around 1941, just before America joined the fighting in World War II.
Photo provided by her family.

"We spoke only Gaelic in our house in Ireland and the United States," Kay said in "The Kathleen McNulty Mauchly Antonelli Story," published by her family in

2004. However, when her older brothers started going to school, she eagerly listened in on their studies. After attending schools in Philadelphia and earning good grades, Kay enrolled in Chestnut Hill College and took all sorts of math classes. "I loved it and found it fun and easy to do," she said. "I didn't want to teach. I just wanted to do the math puzzles."

Kay graduated in 1942 with a degree in mathematics. America's involvement with the war had begun just a few months earlier, pulling men out of the workforce and into battle in Europe and the Pacific. This opened up a world of employment possibilities for women like Kay. About two weeks after graduating, Kay saw an ad in a Philadelphia paper looking for female math majors. The job they were asked to do? Serve as "computers."

Kay wasn't the only woman to answer the advertisement— hundreds of women did. But six special mathematicians— Kay and her friend from math class Fran Bilas, along with Jean Jennings, Ruth Lichterman, Betty Snyder, and Marlyn Wescoff—were asked to use their remarkable math skills in service to a top secret, massive new calculator called the ENIAC.

"We knew this calculator was being built at the Moore School," wrote Kay about her work on what came to be known as Project PX, "but nobody talked to us about it, and we really had no idea what it looked like. I never went into the PX room because it was classified 'confidential,' with signs saying that no one without clearance was allowed in the room."

The result of Project PX was the ENIAC, which is considered the world's first electronic, digital, general-purpose computer. It was created by physics professor John W. Mauchly (whom Kay later married) and electrical engineer J. Presper Eckert to speed up the time it took to solve complicated math problems. It could work a thousand times faster than human computers. Through cables, switches, and vacuum tubes set in specific sequences, the ENIAC could calculate a bullet's trajectory faster than it took the bullet to travel. But the trick was arranging it all just right.

With no instructions or manual to guide them, the ENIAC Six had to figure out on their own how to get the machine to do what they wanted. And so with every pattern they set up, they wrote down the precise steps, then unplugged the cables and moved them to another spot. Soon they were doing something that had never been done before: programming!

On February 15, 1946, when the ENIAC was unveiled to the world, newspapers trumpeted it as a "huge mechanical Einstein," with headlines reading DOES 100 YEARS' WORK IN TWO HOURS AND OPENS WAY TO BETTER LIFE. To many, this date is considered the start of the modern Information Age we live in today.

That evening, the men involved in the ENIAC project

went out to a celebratory dinner. However, the women of the ENIAC were not invited. Their roles as the machine's programmers were immediately forgotten. Some photographs of the unveiling edited the women out of the pictures; others ignored their intellectual contributions and identified them simply as "models."

"It felt as if history had been made that day," Jean wrote, "and then it had run over us and left us flat in its tracks."

Jean Jennings in 1946, after the ENIAC was introduced to the world.
Photo provided by her family.

World War II had opened the door for women to enter exciting fields of work. But society's stubborn lack of imagination meant many women's accomplishments were overlooked: People just could not believe or accept what women could achieve.

It took more than fifty years for Kay, Jean, Fran, Marlyn, Betty, and Ruth to receive the honors they were due. In 1997, all six of them were inducted into the Women in Technology International Hall of Fame for the part they played in programming the ENIAC. And since then, more has been done to recognize their roles. Even Grace Hopper, another barrier-breaking computer scientist, once said she considered Betty Snyder to be the best computer programmer she'd ever known.

Jean Jennings (left) and Fran Bilas adjust settings on the ENIAC, whose panels stood eight feet high and length stretched ninety-eight feet. The size of an apartment, ENIAC was the world's first electronic, digital computer and the ENIAC Six the first programmers.
Photo courtesy of the United States Army, via Wikimedia Commons.

"If my life has proven anything, it is that women should never be afraid to take risks and try new things,"

Jean wrote in her autobiography. "Women should pursue their dreams no matter where those dreams may lead them and push into frontiers where women aren't necessarily welcome to shape their own destinies."

You can learn more about the ENIAC Six by visiting documentarian Kathy Kleiman's engaging and informative ENIAC Programmers Project at http://eniacprogrammers .org. And read Kay's own words about the ENIAC and how much she loved math at a website created by her family at https://sites.google.com/a/opgate.com/eniac/Home /kay-mcnulty-mauchly-antonelli.

The Spy Ring

The most extensive spy ring ever to infiltrate the United States was led by Fritz Duquesne (pronounced "du-KANE"), a Nazi intelligence officer who was living and working in the United States just before the start of WWII. His nickname was "the Duke."

With thirty-three members, according to the FBI, the spy ring's goal was to steal military secrets as well as sabotage American factories and infrastructure. The spies, men and a few women, took jobs working for airlines, shipping companies, and defense factories, and more ordinary roles in restaurants.

They blended in to everyday society, but while they

thought they were making inroads, the spies were under constant film surveillance from a hidden camera in a young German colleague's office. The colleague's name was Harry Sawyer, and he hated the Nazis. Harry had volunteered to work as a double agent, helping the FBI shut down the Duke and other members of the spy ring. Harry's real name was William "Bill" Sebold, and he's considered the first American hero of WWII.

For this story, I moved Harry, the Duke, and his spy ring from New York to Philadelphia. But you can learn more of the facts about the real-life case in the FBI's archives at https://www.fbi.gov/history/famous-cases /duquesne-spy-ring. Or watch FBI archival footage of the Duquesne spy ring and other wartime military propaganda online at the United States Holocaust Memorial Museum at https://collections.ushmm.org/search/catalog /irn1003974.

Radio News Reports

You can listen to President Roosevelt's radio address to Congress and the nation the day after the Japanese attacked Pearl Harbor, in what has come to be known as the "Date of Infamy" speech, at https://www.nationalgeographic.org /media/roosevelts-day-infamy-speech/.

Or listen to other WWII radio news reports to get a sense of what Americans back home learned of the war's progress at websites such as the World War II Foundation at www .wwiifoundation.org/students/real-time-radio-broadcasts -from-d-day-june-6-1944/.

RECOMMENDED RESOURCES

Books

Bartik, Jean Jennings. *Pioneer Programmer: Jean Jennings Bartik and the Computer that Changed the World.* Kirksville, MO: Truman State University Press, 2013.

Benton, Mike. *Superhero Comics of the Golden Age: The Illustrated History.* Dallas, TX: Taylor, 1992.

Cahan, Richard, and Michael Williams. *Un-American: The Incarceration of Japanese Americans During World War II.* Chicago: CityFiles Press, 2016.

Coogan, Peter. *Superhero: The Secret Origin of a Genre.* Austin, TX: MonkeyBrain Books, 2006.

Duffy, Peter. *Double Agent: The First Hero of World War II and How the FBI Outwitted and Destroyed a Nazi Spy Ring.* New York: Scribner, 2014.

King, Bart, and Greg Paprocki. *The Big Book of Superheroes.* Layton, UT: Gibbs Smith, 2014.

Lepore, Jill. *The Secret History of Wonder Woman.* New York: Knopf, 2014.

Lindop, Edmund, wiht Margaret J. Goldstein. *America in the 1940s.* Minneapolis, MN. Twenty-First Century Books, 2009.

Madrid, Mike. *Divas, Dames & Daredevils: Lost Heroines of Golden Age Comics.* Ashland, OR: Exterminating Angel Press, 2013.

Madrid, Mike. *The Supergirls: Fashion, Feminism, Fantasy, and the History of Comic Book Heroines.* Ashland, OR: Exterminating Angel Press, 2009.

Maslon, Laurence, and Michael Kantor. *Superheroes! Capes, Cowls, and the Creation of Comic Book Culture.* New York: Crown Archetype, 2013.

Robbins, Trina. The Great Women Cartoonists. New York: Watson-Guptill, 2001.

Robbins, Trina. *The Great Women Superheroes.* Northampton, MA: Kitchen Sink Press, 1996.

Robbins, Trina. Pretty in Ink: North American Women Cartoonists 1896–2013. Seattle: Fantagraphics Books, 2013.

Documentaries

The Computers: The Remarkable Story of the ENIAC Programmers.
Directed by Kathy Kleiman, Kate McMahon, and
Jon Palfreman. ENIAC Programmers Project:
eniacprogrammers.org, 2016.

Top Secret Rosies: The Female "Computers" of WWII. Directed by
LeAnn Erickson. Written by Cynthia Baughman. PBS,
2010.

Wonder Women! The Untold Story of American Superheroines.
Directed by Kristy Guevara-Flanagan. Performed by
Lynda Carter, Lindsay Wagner. Produced by Kelcey
Edwards, 2012.

Websites

"Duquesne Spy Ring." FBI. Accessed May 18, 2016.
https://www.fbi.gov/history/famous-cases/duquesne-spy
-ring.

"The Kathleen McNulty Mauchly Antonelli Story." Google
Sites. https://sitesgoogle.com/a/opgate.com/eniac/Home
/kay-mcnulty-mauchly-antonelli.

ACKNOWLEDGMENTS

$\mathcal{K}$AY MCNULTY, JEAN JENNINGS, AND THE other ENIAC programmers featured in *Cape* were exciting figures, and I am thankful to have corresponded with their children. Eva Mauchly, Bill Mauchly, and Gini Mauchly Calcerano were spectacular storytellers who generously shared details about their mother, Kay—from her height and eye color to the way she told jokes, how she couldn't really sing, and that she devoted a good part of her life to the Girl Scouts. I'm also grateful to Jean's children—Tim Bartik, Jane Bartik, and Mary Williams—who generously shared details with me about their amazing mother, including her "fire-engine-red hair."

Thanks also to fellow authors and helpful early readers Franny Billingsley and Dana Alison Levy; to comic book gurus Sam Hopkins and James Nurss of First Aid Comics in Chicago; to my local public library's children's librarian and reading superhero Tina Carter; to documentarian Kathy Kleiman; to the ever-patient and always-positive Jennifer Mattson and Naoum Issa; and to my brother-in-law Philip Issa for his help on superhero world-building, as well as for asking the exact right questions.

I am grateful to the legendary Trina Robbins, who has been writing and drawing comics and graphic novels for more than forty years, for sitting down with me to talk about early superheroes and the best superpowers. And I thank my sister-in-law Suzy Nakamura, who shared her mother's experience coming of age in a Japanese internment camp in Minidoka, Idaho, and her father's in Manzanar, California. Thanks also to Takayo Fischer, who generously talked to me about her own experiences as a young girl in internment camps in Jerome and Rohwer, Arkansas.

ABOUT THE AUTHOR

$\mathcal{K}$ATE HANNIGAN writes fiction and nonfiction for young readers, and she especially loves digging up remarkable people from history and sharing their stories. Her superpower seems to be parallel parking, but if she could choose, it would be teleportation. She lives in Chicago with her husband, three kids, and an anxious Australian shepherd. Learn more about WWII superheroes at KateHannigan.com.